I0773302

Also by the Author

The Erin O'Reilly Mysteries

Black Velvet
Irish Car Bomb
White Russian
Double Scotch
Manhattan
Black Magic
Death By Chocolate
Massacre
Flashback

First Love
High Stakes
Aquarium
The Devil You Know
Hair of the Dog
Punch Drunk
Bossa Nova
Blackout
Angel Face

Fathers
A Modern Christmas Story

The Clarion Chronicles
Ember of Dreams

Tequila Sunrise

A James Corcoran Story

Steven Henry

Clickworks Press • Baltimore, MD

First publication: Clickworks Press, 2023
Release: CWP-EORJC1-INT-P.IS-1.0

Sign up for updates, deals, and exclusive sneak peeks at clickworkspress.com/join.

Ebook ISBN: 979-8-88900-002-0
Paperback ISBN: 979-8-88900-003-7
Hardcover ISBN: 979-8-88900-004-4

For all those who choose hope and love
in spite of pain and fear.

Tequila Sunrise

Stir or shake together 1.5 oz. tequila and ¾ cup fresh-squeezed orange juice. Fill a 12-oz. glass with ice cubes. Pour mixture into glass. Slowly add 1.5 oz. grenadine, allowing it to settle to the bottom of the glass (this takes a little while). Garnish with a maraschino cherry and an orange slice.

"Now boarding, all rows, flight 8396 to JFK."

She reminded herself to stand up straight, to look the ticket agent in the eye. She mustn't act like she had anything to hide. He'd told her, "When you're trying to get away with something, the one thing you can't do is look guilty. Be a perfect angel on the outside."

She didn't feel angelic. But maybe determination was a good enough substitute. She hefted her suitcase in one hand and started forward. In her other hand she clutched her boarding pass.

The woman at the gate was a stout black woman with a nice smile. The smile made her feel a little better. She handed over the pass. The woman flicked it across the electronic scanner, the machine beeped, and then the airline worker was handing it back to her, still smiling.

"Enjoy your flight, Ms. Lopez."

"Thank you," she said. And just like that, she was on the plane.

She had a window seat. As the plane taxied onto the runway, she stared out into the night. She realized she was chewing on her lower lip and told herself to stop. There was nothing to worry about. Everything was going according to plan.

But she felt so very alone.

The flight attendant gave the demonstration of how to put on the seatbelt and told them what to do if the cabin depressurized. None of that seemed terribly important, compared with what she was leaving behind, and what she was going to meet. A little thing like being unable to breathe at 30,000 feet was trivial.

Then the engines roared and an invisible hand pressed her back into her seat. The ground fell away beneath her, the pressure change making her ears pop. With amazing speed, San Diego became a distant field of tiny, twinkling lights.

She let out a breath she hadn't known she was holding and tried to relax her grip on the armrests.

A gray-haired woman had the seat next to her. She had a grandmotherly look. She smiled in a kindly way.

"First time flying, dear?"

"Perdon?"

"Oh, I'm sorry, dear," the old woman said. "I don't speak Spanish. Uh... no habla Espanol?"

"It is all right," she said, trying to put the right accent on the words. "I have a little English. This is my first time in an airplane by myself."

"It's not so bad, dear," the woman said. "After all, you're hardly by yourself. Look around you."

She shouldn't talk much. It might blow her cover. But she remembered, the best way to blend in was to be natural. She wondered how he managed it, how he made it look so easy. She wished he was there with her. But then, if he was, she wouldn't be on the plane in the first place.

"Even a crowd can be lonesome," she said. "If you do not know anyone."

"Well then, dear, I'm Norma Malecek," the old woman said, offering a hand. "Now you know someone."

"Elena Lopez." She shook the hand. It was old and wrinkled, with liver spots speckling the flesh.

"I'm going to see my grandson and his wife," Norma said. "They're expecting their first. Do I look old enough to be a great-grandmother?"

"No!" she exclaimed, putting a hand to her mouth with just the right amount of shocked disbelief. He would have been proud of her acting.

"It'll be a wonderful visit. I've been looking forward to it ever since the wedding. Do you have family in New York, Elena?"

She almost said yes, but caught herself. "There is... a job for me to do there. And..." she hesitated and felt a tingle of blood in her cheeks. "A man."

Norma smiled broadly. "Oh, that's lovely! What's his name?"

"James." There couldn't be any harm in telling that much, surely. It was a common name.

"He must be very special, for you to be taking your first solo flight to see him."

"Yes, he is, how do you say... one in a million."

"Is he a New Yorker?"

"He is... from somewhere else. But he lives in New York."

"How did the two of you meet?"

"It is a long story."

"Well, dear, it's a long flight, and it's hard for me to see my knitting with the lights turned down. My eyes aren't what they used to be. Humor an old lady, Elena Lopez. Tell me a story."

She wondered how much of the truth she dared tell. To start with, her name wasn't Elena Lopez. And she wasn't from Mexico. She was from Brooklyn. She'd met James outside a hotel. It had been nighttime, and it had been raining.

Chapter 1

"Open up, guys. This is O'Reilly."

The voice was female, tough and businesslike. One of the Marshals, Calley, went to the door. He pulled his gun and held it in one hand as he glanced through the peephole.

"What's happened, Detective?" Calley asked.

The Marshals' room adjoined Teresa's. They'd left the connecting door open. Teresa came to the passage between the rooms and stood there, fighting down a rush of fear. Her heart was pounding.

"We don't have much time," Detective O'Reilly said through the outer door. "I'm the only one out here. Open the door."

Calley slid back the bolt and detached the chain-lock. He opened the door, but didn't put his gun away. Its muzzle was pointed at the floor.

"Jesus, Calley, it's me," O'Reilly said. "Careful there."

"What's up?" Calley asked.

"I got word from a guy I know on the street," she said. "Vitelli's heard about Teresa. He knows where she is."

"Bullshit," Calley growled. "Nobody knows we're here. I kept this under tight wraps."

O'Reilly shook her head. "They know."

"Then you were followed," said the other Marshal, the big one, Hodges.

"I don't think so," O'Reilly said. "But it doesn't matter how they know. They're planning something. It's going to go down soon. I can get her out, but she has to go right now."

Teresa cleared her throat, trying to get rid of the dry, sandpapery feeling in her mouth. The Marshals and O'Reilly glanced at her.

"Are they coming for me?" she asked. Her voice trembled.

"Our best bet is to bunker up here," Calley said. "And call for backup."

"This hotel's full of civilians," O'Reilly said. "If there's a shootout, people are going to get hit. These guys have access to military weapons, Calley. Remember what happened with Alfie Madonna? This'll be worse."

Calley hesitated. He was new to his command position and it showed on his face. Teresa wondered how old he was. He couldn't be more than thirty, younger than she was.

"I don't like it," he said. "She's my responsibility."

"Mine, too," O'Reilly said. "I got her into this. I'll get her out of it."

"You're taking her out of WitSec?" Calley demanded. He didn't like it.

O'Reilly nodded. "We're getting out of town right here, tonight," she said. "I know a place she can lie low while we sort out all these damn security leaks."

Calley made up his mind. "Okay. We'll come with you."

"Just as far as the front door," O'Reilly said. "The more guys we have, the greater the chance we'll be noticed. And it's better if none of your people know where we're going."

"What're you implying?" Hodges demanded, bristling.

"All I know is, info about witnesses keeps getting out,"

O'Reilly said. "We can't take chances. Get your coat and shoes, Teresa."

Teresa nodded. She didn't say anything. What was there to say? She retreated into the adjoining room. She could still hear the others talking as she put on her shoes, but her own blood was thundering in her ears and she couldn't make any of it out. She looked doubtfully at the bulky bulletproof vest the Marshals had given her. It went over her head and attached under each arm with Velcro straps. The last time she'd worn Velcro before the vest, she'd been ten years old and had been wearing sneakers. She picked up the robin's-egg raincoat her mom had given her and slipped her arms into the sleeves as she returned to the other room. Almost as an afterthought, she grabbed her purse.

"Ms. Tommasino?" O'Reilly asked.

"Yes?" she managed to say.

"It's time to go. Are you ready?"

Teresa gave a last look around the room. She hadn't brought much with her, and where she was going, she didn't think she'd need anything else. She gripped her purse and nodded.

"Let's go," O'Reilly said.

"We'll go first," Calley said. He nodded to Hodges. "Get the elevator. I'm right behind you."

The big Marshal left the room. Calley followed. O'Reilly paused for a few seconds, then fell in step beside Teresa.

"You clear on the plan?" O'Reilly asked her in a low voice.

"I think so," Teresa said.

"Hey, it's going to be okay," O'Reilly said. Then, in a very soft whisper, "You'll go out to the car, just like we discussed, get in the back seat, make the change, and get out the other side. There'll be a gray Corolla waiting in the lot, just a few yards from you. Don't stop, don't look, and *don't run*. Got it?"

Teresa nodded. Her jaw was very tight.

"Okay," O'Reilly said more loudly, no longer guarding her voice. "The rain will help. It'll make it harder for anyone watching. Let's do this."

Teresa noticed how the detective stepped back and put a hand on her gun as the elevator carriage arrived and the doors slid open. Calley hadn't even holstered his own sidearm. Everyone was tense.

The elevator seemed to take forever to reach ground level. When it finally slowed and stopped, O'Reilly had her hand on her pistol again. But the lobby was empty except for the man at the desk. He raised his eyebrows at the officers, who ignored him.

They crossed the lobby. Teresa saw the rain falling outside. Only the little patch of sidewalk under the awning was dry. She started to pull up her raincoat's hood.

"No," O'Reilly said quietly, motioning with her hand. Teresa obediently let the hood fall back to her shoulders. She felt terribly exposed, but maybe that was the point. People were supposed to see her get into the car.

The car was a black sport-utility vehicle, the windows tinted dark. With the night and the rain, it was impossible to see if anyone was inside. A black Lincoln Towncar pulled up behind it. That would be the Marshals' vehicle. Calley and Hodges moved apart, Hodges walking quickly to the front of the SUV and Calley covering the rear.

Teresa hesitated. She couldn't help it. Something awful was about to happen.

"Keep moving," O'Reilly said softly. She reached out and opened the back door of the car. Its inside light didn't turn on; Teresa realized they must have disabled it. She swallowed and stepped across the sidewalk to the curb. Then she tucked her raincoat up around her legs and climbed in. O'Reilly swung the door shut behind her.

Teresa's heart almost stopped. Someone was already in the back seat, an immobile form that radiated cold. She couldn't make out the details of the face, but she was grateful for that. Just wriggling past that horrible, stiff body was almost more than she could do.

But if she didn't, she would be killed. She knew that, beyond a doubt. The only way out was through. And she had to move quickly. She took a breath, clamped her teeth on her lip to stifle any involuntary cry, and looped the strap of her purse around one stiff, cold hand. A coat and hat were on the seat next to the body. She squirmed into the coat, putting it on over her raincoat, and clamped the hat on her own head. It was a police Patrolman's hat, many-sided. She pulled it as low over her forehead as she could.

"Calley!" O'Reilly shouted. "Six o'clock!"

O'Reilly was standing behind the SUV, pointing at something behind the Lincoln. Teresa saw a vague, menacing shape in the rain. It looked like a man, a very large one.

She had to keep to the plan, had no choice but to trust O'Reilly. She opened the far door of the car and stepped out into the rain again. She shut the door behind her, remembering the way they'd talked about it, and started walking.

Without looking back, she began crossing the parking lot, though she couldn't see the car she was supposed to go to. The rain brought the night in very close. Raindrops drummed on her hat, pattered against her borrowed coat, and caught in her eyelashes. Cold rain splashed her face.

This was never going to work, Teresa told herself, even as she was looking for a gray Corolla. It would never fool the men who were chasing her. Never, never, never. They were too smart, too dangerous.

There was the gray car, parked exactly where it was supposed to be. She took a step toward it, then another.

Behind her, the SUV exploded.

There was a brilliant red-gold flash and a tremendous noise. A boiling cloud of heat rolled against her back. She was momentarily deafened by the roar of the blast. Raindrops hissed and steamed silently. The glass awning in front of the hotel flew apart, erupting upward like some strange transparent volcano. Pieces of metal and glass, hurled high into the air, began to fall back to the parking lot. There were pieces of something else, too, something dreadful.

"Walk, don't run," O'Reilly had said. It was the hardest thing Teresa had ever done, but she did it, walking briskly to the parked car, not looking back. Someone was screaming somewhere, it seemed very far away.

The driver's door of the Corolla was open. A man got out. Teresa caught a quick glimpse of a smiling, pleasant face, of red, curly hair under a police cap. The man moved very fast, but gracefully, gliding to the passenger door and swinging it open for her.

She got in. He closed the door almost before she was seated, and in a matter of seconds he was in the driver's seat. The engine was already running. He put the car in gear and drove.

As they pulled out of the parking space, Teresa risked a look toward the car that should have taken her to the courthouse. It looked like it had been struck by an aerial bomb. Flames shot toward the sky out of the wreckage. Teresa caught a glimpse of Detective O'Reilly and the other three police officers. They had guns in their hands and were shouting something. They didn't seem to be hurt. Teresa was glad.

"Well," the driver of her car said, his voice cutting through the ringing in her ears. "That was a fine close shave, wasn't it, love?" His accent was unmistakably that of an Irishman.

"Yes," Teresa said, hoping her voice wouldn't shake too badly. It did.

"I'm James," he said. "I'd offer to shake hands, but seeing as how we're in the midst of a death-defying escape, perhaps we'd best wait for a more opportune moment. You're not hurt, are you?"

"No," she said quietly. "I'm... I'm Teresa."

"Of course you are, love," he said. "And you needn't fear. Everything's gone precisely to plan."

"I didn't think it would be... so... so..."

"Dramatic?" he offered.

"Yes."

James laughed. "Ah, that'd be my mate's doing. There's no better hand with a car bomb. I could tell you some stories about him." He glanced sidelong at her and thought better of it. "Another time, maybe. For now, let's get you off Long Island. We've a long way to go, and plenty of time for talking."

*   *   *

Teresa didn't feel much like talking. She was still shaken by the explosion. But James was more than willing to fill up the silence. He was the most talkative police officer she'd ever met. Most of his conversation was in the form of humorous anecdotes, usually prompted by a location they passed. He seemed to know Brooklyn very well. Every street, every landmark had a story associated with it.

"Now love, there's a bowling alley down that way," he said as they passed the 39th Street exit on 278. "I knew a lad who used to bowl there every Thursday. Worst bowler you ever knew. This lad couldn't buy a spare at discount on clearance. But he kept coming to the lanes, kept bowling scores that would shame a football team. Finally, one night, one of the other lads says to him, 'Donny, lad, I love you like a brother, but I swear, you're the worst bowler on God's green Earth. Why do you keep coming here?'

"Donny, he takes a long, slow look at his friend and says, 'I know it, lad. But this is my old lady's bridge night.'

"'What's that to do with it?' asks the other lad.

"'Well, we've a bit of a wager on the evening,' says Donny. 'If I win at the bowling, then she's to do whatever I'm wanting in the bedroom. If she wins at the bridge, then I'm to do whatever she's wanting, turnabout and fair play.'

"The other lad still doesn't get it. 'But Donny,' he says, 'why aren't you trying to win, then?'

"Donny gives him another long look. 'Lad,' he says, 'you've not seen my wife, have you? Why do you think I want to get out of the house every Thursday?'

"'But what about her? Don't you still have to give her what she's wanting, when she wins?'

"'Nay, lad,' Donny says, and now he's looking confused. 'For some reason, since we made the wager, she's never won a rubber of bridge. I swear, that woman's got the worst luck in the world!'"

Teresa gave him the best smile she could manage. "Officer?"

"Please, love, don't be calling me that."

"Oh, right," she said, feeling embarrassed. They were undercover, in witness protection. She'd have to get used to plainclothes cops. He'd already tossed his policeman's hat into the back seat, revealing a full head of curly, flaming red hair. "What should I call you, then?"

"James is my name, as I've told you. But my mates call me Corky."

"All right... James," she said. "Excuse me, but I don't know where we're going."

"Ah, you needn't trouble about that. We're making for the Narrows, across to Staten Island. We'll change in a little place on Emerson Hill, then it's New Jersey for us. Once we've crossed the state line, we'll breathe a mite easier. I've a hotel lined up."

"And after that?"

"We'll keep driving, love. Far as we need, until we're in the clear. I'm thinking Mexico."

"Mexico?" she exclaimed. "That's hundreds of miles! It's all the way across the country!"

He grinned. "Aye, it's a tidy way, to be sure. But we'll see how we go. Day at a time, that's the best way to live, love."

Teresa fell silent. Staten Island was far enough for her, New Jersey a serious adventure. Mexico might as well be on the far side of the planet.

"You know, love," James said as they rolled toward the Verrazzano-Narrows Bridge, "you're forbidden to take pictures on this bridge."

"Why's that?" she asked.

"They're worried about terrorists, of course. Why else?"

"Terrorists," she repeated.

"Aye." He slowed down, drumming his fingers on the steering wheel. Traffic was thickening up. "Know what I think? It's these bloody tollbooths. If I had to drive this route every day, I'd want to blow the bridge up myself, just to get rid of them. You haven't any change about you, have you?"

"What? Um, no." She didn't have even a single dollar in her pockets, not since she'd left her purse in the other car. She wouldn't be seeing that purse again, that was for sure.

"No fear, love," he said, grinning again. "I'm just teasing. I've plenty of scratch to see us where we need to go."

The traffic jam caused by the tollbooths made Teresa nervous. She kept glancing in the rear-view mirror, wondering whether the Mafia had guys following them. She remembered that famous scene from *The Godfather*, the one where Sonny got gunned down at the tollbooth. She looked at James out of the corner of her eye. He didn't seem worried. He'd already started another of his stories. She was only half listening, thinking what she'd do if gunmen showed up. Should she run, or stick close to him?

"Is it safe?" she asked abruptly.

"What's troubling you, love?" he asked, breaking off his story mid-sentence.

"Here," she said, waving a hand vaguely at the cars around them. "I mean, couldn't there be... men following us?"

"Nay, love," he said. "If we'd been tailed, I'd know it. Don't fret. I swear, I'll let no harm come to you. If those Mafia bastards chase after you, I'll protect you. But first they'll have to find us."

"You've got a gun. Don't you?"

He looked at her and smiled, but his eyes were softer than she'd seen before. "I can see you're frightened. As God's my witness, you're safe with me. Do you believe me?"

Strangely, she did. Something about James made her feel that he could carry her past any danger, through any trouble. His careless, easy manner gave her a security she hadn't felt ever since she'd seen those awful men in her apartment, back when the nightmare had begun.

The cars crawled forward, agonizingly slowly. James started singing softly. He had a good voice, a pleasant tenor.

"Now, when I was a young man, I lived near the sea-strand,
And me folks kept a tavern called the Admiral's Head.
And old salts by the fireside would tell of the seas wide,
The far foreign shores, and the lives that they'd led.
And it's up and away in the morning,
For the tears me poor mother has cried,
And you may think I'm balmy, but the sea she had called me,
And I went to her just like a bride.
And it's up and away in the morning..."

Teresa listened through that song, and two more, before their turn finally came at the tollbooth. James had the necessary thirteen dollars ready, peeled off a roll from his pocket. He flashed the toll-taker a brilliant smile and accelerated through the gate and across the Narrows to Staten Island.

As Brooklyn receded behind them and disappeared into the rainy dark, Teresa took a deep breath and settled back in her seat. She looked at the luminous dial of her wristwatch. Not even ten o' clock yet. The night felt like it was never going to end.

Chapter 2

Emerson Hill was a quiet neighborhood, with small houses nestled behind gated driveways. James drove the Corolla up to a darkened house. He jumped out of the car, leaving the engine running, and opened the gate. He pulled inside into a two-car garage, next to a dark red Honda Accord.

"Right, love," he said, stopping the Corolla and opening the driver's door. "There's a bag in the back seat. Take off that coat you're wearing, and the hat. The vest, too. Leave them here."

Teresa did as instructed, thinking of the robin's-egg coat she'd left in the car with the body. She'd been slowly stripping away her own identity, a little bit at a time, and even a little thing like a raincoat hurt to leave behind. She remembered the day she'd bought it, shopping with her mother, three years ago. Maybe she'd never see her mom again.

Taking off the bulletproof vest felt better. It had been heavy, dragging her down with its promise of bulky protection. The fact of its removal told her she was safer than she had been. She hoped it wasn't an illusion.

James was watching her, looking her over. Teresa felt suddenly self-conscious. She was wearing a plain, conservative white blouse with gray slacks and low, conservative heels on her feet. It was hardly an eye-catching ensemble. But still, being examined by men had always made her a little nervous. She fought the urge to cross her arms over her chest, reminding herself that James was her protector. She was in no danger from him.

He smiled. "There's a coat for you in the bag. Put it on." He'd already taken off his own jacket. Underneath, he had on a dark green shirt that looked like silk, open at the neck. "When you've done," he added, "there's another for me. If you'd be so kind?"

She found a women's coat, black, brand new. It came down to mid-thigh on her, fitting perfectly.

"I hope I had your measurements right," he said.

"This is fine," she said, handing him the black sport coat from the bottom of the duffel bag.

He tossed the coat on, not bothering to button it. "Right, then. Let's be off. We've just a few more miles to cover tonight, then to bed." He dropped the Corolla's keys onto the driver's seat, drew a second set of keys out of his pocket, and unlocked the Accord.

Soon they were back on 278 in their new car, westbound across Staten Island. James began his running commentary again, this time with a story of a lost cat that had somehow ended up in a long-haul trucker's trailer and ridden all the way to Denver before being discovered.

"By the time the lad got back to New York," James finished, "he'd grown so used to the cat that before looking up the owner, he went to a pet store."

"And bought himself a cat?" Teresa guessed. "That's sweet."

"Nay," James said. "He looked for another cat with the same coloring and switched out the collars."

"He didn't!"

"Aye," he laughed. "He gave the wrong cat back and kept the stowaway."

"But the owner must have noticed the difference!"

"Aye," James said thoughtfully. "The original owner was a mite confused. It seems he'd had the poor girl fixed, so no one was more surprised than he when a litter of kittens arrived the following year. But he made a profit selling them, so there was no harm done in the end."

"James!"

"Aye, love?"

"Are you making that up?"

"I'm a terrible liar," he said.

"Do you mean you're bad at lying, or you're terrible because you lie?"

He grinned. "I don't like to lie to a pretty lass. Thus far, every word to you's been God's honest truth."

"Unless you're lying about that," she said.

"Aye," he said cheerfully. "In which case, I fear you're left to draw your own conclusions."

*　*　*

Their endpoint for the night was a Hampton Inn situated in Linden, New Jersey, a place Teresa had never been, nor even heard of. It had the comforting familiarity of large hotel chains, a clean, anonymous feel. Teresa tried to think of the whole situation as nothing more than a cross-country trip, like she'd often talked about making with her parents but never gotten around to doing.

James led her straight into the hotel, past the lobby without stopping. At the elevators, she caught up to him and took hold of his arm.

"Don't we need to check in?"

He laid a hand on hers. It was the first time he'd touched her. His hand was warm, his touch surprisingly gentle. "Nay, love, I took care of that already." He patted his breast pocket. "I've the room key here. We're under a name that's not yours, never fear."

"We?" she echoed. She felt her eyebrows draw together. "But..."

"Aye," he said pleasantly. The elevator doors opened. He stepped in, and she had no choice but to follow. "How else am I to keep an eye on you, make sure you're safe?"

She spent the ride to the third floor trying to figure out what to say, and not coming up with anything.

"Here we are, 315," he said. He unlocked the door and flicked on the lights. "All the comforts of home."

Teresa hesitated in the doorway. "Is... is it safe?" she asked. She'd been expecting him to clear the room, like she'd seen on TV.

"Love," he said, "we're in a room for which I've paid cash, under a false name. If any lad knows we're here, and has been lying in wait, we're already in such trouble it'll scarcely matter if I find him or not. But if it'll set your mind easy, I'll take a look." He poked his head into the bathroom, checked the closet, and even ducked to peer under the beds.

"Not a hitman in sight," he announced, popping back up with a grin.

She gave him a tired smile. "Thank you, James. And thank you for being patient with me. I'm... not used to this. I don't mean to be difficult."

"Ah, love," he said, giving her that brilliant, dazzling smile. "Think nothing of it. I'm very much at your service. Is there anything you're requiring?"

"I just want to get clean and dry," she said. "And try to sleep. I'm exhausted."

"Grand."

"But..."

"Aye?"

"I don't have anything to wear except what I've got on."

His smile didn't falter. "Not to worry. I've arranged some things for you. None of your own clothes, I fear. That would have looked suspicious. But Erin told me to get you some traveling clothes. There's a bag in the closet. I'll just let you take care of yourself in the bathroom. I'll be right outside should you need anything."

She took the overnight bag from the closet into the bathroom with her, closing the door behind her and, after a moment's thought, locking it. It wasn't that she didn't trust James personally. She was just having a hard time trusting anyone or anything right then.

The hot water felt absolutely marvelous, cascading over her head and shoulders. She stood there and soaked in it for a long while, trying to wash away her worries. It didn't completely work, but she did feel better when she finally turned off the shower. She toweled off and dried her hair as best she could. It was thick and wavy, and really needed a blow-dryer, but she couldn't be too picky. In the travel bag James had provided, she found a long T-shirt that would serve as a nightshirt. But she didn't find any pajama pants. Apparently that had been overlooked. There were a pair of slacks and two pairs of blue jeans, but those were no good to sleep in.

Teresa considered her options. The shirt was long enough for the bare needs of modesty, as long as she didn't sit down facing another person. That would have to do. She pulled on a fresh pair of underwear, a little different from her usual style but not uncomfortable. She imagined James standing in Victoria's Secret picking out panties, and felt herself blush a little. Shaking the thought away, she told herself to stop being a silly, prudish girl. She was thirty-four years old, a schoolteacher who could call a roomful of rambunctious kids to order with a single stern word. She was not going to let herself be embarrassed by a little thing like the fact that she wasn't wearing any pants.

She took a deep breath and opened the bathroom door. "All right, James," she said. "Bathroom's free."

She stepped out into the bedroom, fighting the urge to grab the bottom of her T-shirt and pull it lower on her legs. James was sitting on the near bed. He smiled warmly at her, and she knew he was noticing her legs. She'd dealt with the stares of men before, but this man affected her differently. Maybe it was the unusual situation, the tension of the day. But he didn't seem creepy. His appreciative glance just made her feel warm and confused. Besides, he was mostly looking at her face.

He stood up and stepped toward her. "Thanks, love," he said. "I'll just clean myself up, then, and we'll be getting to bed."

For a single wild moment, he paused and she thought he was going to put a hand on her shoulder, touch her, maybe even kiss her. But of course he didn't. He walked past her, his hand brushing against her side in the narrow space by the bathroom door. He was unbuttoning his shirt as he went, and she told herself again to stop being silly. He obviously didn't consider it any big deal to be changing clothes around her. It was nothing. James was a professional. She was safe.

He didn't close the bathroom door. After a minute or so, she heard the shower start up again. Of course, Teresa thought. He needed to hear if anything happened, if she needed help. But she still got into bed hurriedly and pulled the comforter up to her neck. She felt better once she was covered up, more in control of things. She turned out the bedroom light.

The shower eventually stopped. Teresa saw a shadow fall across the room from the bathroom. She wondered what he was wearing. It wasn't any of her business, she told herself, but she still almost turned over to check.

"Good night, love," James said quietly. "You're a brave lass, you know. You've been brilliant. Everything's going to be fine."

She tried to believe him, and almost did. But it was a long time before she was able to relax enough to fall asleep.

*   *   *

"We've reached our cruising altitude," the pilot said over the plane's intercom. "We expect a smooth flight to New York. We've turned off the seat belt light, so you can get up and move around the cabin. However, we ask that you keep your belts fastened when you're seated. Your flight attendants will be passing out refreshments shortly. Sit back, relax, and enjoy your flight."

"James was on a business trip," Teresa told Norma.

"What kind of business is he in, dear?"

"Shipping."

James would be proud of that answer, she thought. "The best way to lie," he'd told her, "is to tell a particular kind of truth. Let the other lad fill in the blanks."

Norma nodded. "That's nice, dear. Was it love at first sight?"

Teresa smiled. "Not exactly. I liked the looks of him, I suppose, and he certainly liked me. But it wasn't like that. I wasn't thinking of him that way. And there were... complications."

Chapter 3

Teresa's ears rang with the blast of the car bomb. Flaming debris rained down around her, a hellish hail of fire, steel, and rain.

Her eyes flew open and she cried out. She didn't know where she was. She sat up, gasped in a breath, and stared wildly around.

"What's the matter, love?"

A lightbulb flared. Teresa's half-imagined fears and nightmares scattered. She saw the hotel room, so ordinary and recognizable, and remembered where she was. She sagged back against the headboard. The sheets and comforter were rumpled where she'd thrashed around in her sleep. She rubbed her eyes and looked across the room to the other bed.

There was James. He'd rolled out of bed when she'd screamed. He was standing in the middle of the room, clad only in a pair of boxer shorts. His hair was a red, curly mess, but he looked wide-eyed and awake. One hand hovered near the light switch. The other held a silver, shiny thing.

"I'm all right," she said. "Just... just a bad dream."

"Ah," he said. "Grand." He did something with his right hand as he stepped back toward his bed. The silver thing folded up into itself and disappeared under his pillow.

"What've you got there?" she asked.

"You needn't concern yourself with that, love," he said with a pleasant grin. "I hope you weren't thinking of the unpleasantness yesterday." On the table between the beds, a digital clock read 03:16. If he was upset at being woken in the middle of the night, he didn't give any sign of it.

She swallowed. "I can't think of anything else."

He nodded. "Aye, it's a rare thing, and a bit upsetting the first time or two you see it. But there's no harm done."

"No harm?" she echoed, staring at him in disbelief. "They *blew up a car!* With a dead body inside!"

"Aye, that was the plan. Didn't Erin explain it to you?"

"Well... yes. But I didn't think..." She shuddered and rubbed her hands together. "I touched... it. In the car. It was so *cold.*"

"I understand they retrieved her from the city morgue," he said. "A fair match, I'm told. Quite the resemblance. Not that it matters, given the current state of things. The whole point of using a bomb was to render the body unrecognizable. Lass, you've a death order on you, you know that. In order to get out from under it, you've got to seem to be dead."

"I understand, James. But... but... I can't... can't..." She waved her hands helplessly. "It was horrible!"

James nodded sympathetically. "Aye, love, it's hard luck on you. But you're well out of it now. Not a soul knows where we've gone, I made certain of that."

"No one? Not Detective O'Reilly, even?"

He smiled. "We were very specific on the point. We're to disappear. Mexico's my own plan and Erin knows nothing of it. I've handled the identity papers, everything. You've nothing to worry about."

She studied him more closely than before. His age was hard to place. He might be thirty, or fifty, or anything in between. His eyes had a bright sparkle that suggested youth, but the laugh lines around them hinted at years of accumulated experience. He was slim and in good shape; not much hair on his chest; a flat, well-muscled stomach. She couldn't help noticing his mostly-bare body and seeing a man who took care of himself. He had a tattoo on his shoulder; a fancy Celtic design full of intertwining knots. Several scars scattered his torso.

She looked back at his face. One eyebrow was raised. James looked amused.

"Do you like what you see, love?"

Teresa's cheeks tingled. "Aren't you getting cold, standing there like that?"

"Nay, I run hot. Can I get you anything, while I'm up? A glass of water, maybe? Or if you've a need for something stronger, I've a flask."

"A flask of what?" she asked with sudden suspicion.

"Milk, of course."

"Won't it have gone off, sitting at room temp?"

He turned to the chair, where he'd draped his trousers, and fished a hip flask out of the pocket. He casually tossed it to her. Startled, she fumbled the catch. The flask tumbled through her hands. She retrieved it from the pile of bedclothes and unscrewed the top. She sniffed the mouthpiece.

"James, that's not milk!"

"Mother's milk," he said, still grinning. "The very finest, all the way from Scotland. Glen Docherty-Kinlochewe. A sure cure for bad dreams, love. Have a wee nip."

She doubtfully raised the flask and took a very small sip. She blinked and reflexively coughed. Fierce heat flowed down her throat and up through the roof of her mouth. Her eyes watered. "What on earth?" she gasped.

He crossed the room in three easy strides and sat down on the edge of her bed. "Easy, love," he said. His brow crinkled. "You've not tasted good Scotch whiskey before?"

"No," she said. "In my family we drink wine, if we have anything alcoholic. I don't drink hard liquor."

He laughed quietly and put a hand on her shoulder. "Easy, love. It's a taste to be acquired. You'll feel better presently."

She took another careful, shaky drink. The heat was a little less intense this time, more of a slow, spreading tingling. After a few moments, she found that she did feel better.

James's hand was still on her shoulder. She felt the warmth of his palm through her shirt. He was telling the truth about running hot, she thought. She put a hand on his, letting it rest there for a moment.

Then it struck her what she was doing. She was sitting in bed, in a hotel room, with a man who was a complete stranger, drinking his whiskey, letting him touch her, while he was wearing more or less nothing.

She thrust the whiskey flask at him with an abruptness that startled both of them. "Thank you, James. I'm all right now."

"Are you certain? If you're needing me to sit up with you a bit longer..."

"No," she said quickly. "I'm fine. We should get some more sleep. We've got a lot of driving tomorrow."

He stood up. As he did, he rotated his hand so he was holding her own in his. He gave her fingers a light squeeze, reassuring and tender. "All right, love," he said quietly. "But if you're needing anything, anything at all, you've only to call."

* * *

Neither of them said anything about the nighttime interlude the following morning. James was as bright-eyed and chipper as if he'd slept ten hours straight. Teresa felt tired and dragged out, a little headachy. It couldn't be the whiskey. She hadn't had nearly enough to be hungover. Maybe life handed out its own hangovers, she thought sourly.

It was hard to stay grumpy around James. He was so constantly cheerful, his spirits lifting hers without apparent effort. Even an early-morning drive through eastern New Jersey didn't dampen his enthusiasm for life. He kept up a steady stream of light chatter, making her smile and even laugh from time to time.

"Why are you doing this, James?" she finally asked. They were making good time down I-95, still a little ahead of rush hour.

"Doing what, love?"

"Helping me."

He glanced at her. "Would you rather I didn't?"

"No! I just... I mean, were you given this assignment? As an order?"

"Oh, nay, I volunteered. Jumped at the call, really."

"Why?"

"Why not?"

Teresa shook her head in confusion. "My whole life is back there." She waved her hand over her shoulder in the general direction of New York. "I didn't want to leave. That's my home. And it's yours, too, isn't it?"

"Oh aye, the Big Apple's been home to me for many a year."

She caught the implication. "Where are you from, before that? Where were you born?"

"Occupied Ireland."

"Occupied?"

He smiled. "Northern Ireland, you'd call it. Belfast."

"What brought you here?"

"Personal troubles, political troubles, and a friend."

"How mysterious."

His smile broadened. "Everyone likes a mystery, love. You'd be disappointed if I told you everything about myself right at the start. Now, as for yourself, I'd guess from your manner of speech that Brooklyn's been mother to you?"

"That's where I was born," she confirmed. "My whole family lives there."

"And you're close with your mum and da, your brothers and sisters?"

She nodded and swallowed a sudden lump in her throat. "Yes... yes. They... I... They'll think I'm..." She couldn't finish.

James's smile softened. "Easy, love," he said gently. "I know, this will hurt them. But it's only till the trial comes round. And it's better they only think you're gone, rather than have the reality of it. Think how happy they'll be when you turn up alive again. A proper miracle. Just imagine, love. You'll be resurrected!"

She managed a sad smile. "Can you always see the bright side of things?"

"It's a sight easier than seeing in the dark, love."

"You're like the smart-aleck boys in my classroom," she said. "An answer for everything."

"What age do you teach?"

"Fourth grade. Nine- and ten-year-olds."

"Ah, I remember those days. The penguins did say I was a right cheeky lad."

"Penguins?"

"Nuns, love."

"You went to a Catholic school?"

"Oh aye. It was either that, or sit in class with the Protestant lads up the street who'd like nothing better than to beat the trousers off a wee Catholic lad. Cars and I had enough trouble with them as it was, and besides, my mum wouldn't have had it otherwise."

"Who's Cars?"

"My best mate. Best friend a lad could have in the world."

She looked at him, watching his profile. "I'll bet the two of you got into all kinds of trouble."

That quick grin came back to his face, like the sun breaking through clouds. "You don't know the half of it, love."

"Why'd you become a policeman?"

He shot her a quick look. "Well, love, a lad with my background's got just two choices, really. It came down to a choice between copper and crook, I suppose, and my choice was an easy one in the end."

"Have you ever done this before?"

"Done what, exactly?"

"Been a... protector?"

"This is the first such job I've done for the city of New York," he said. "But I promise you, I'll not let you down."

*   *   *

They spent the morning on I-95, working their way through New Jersey toward Washington, DC. James mentioned he'd once considered living in Newark.

"Why?" Teresa asked.

"Well, you have to understand, love," he said. "I'd been making some poor decisions at that time of life. And while I've never exactly been the most pious lad, I'd a sort of suspicion I was piling up fire and brimstone for my future."

"And...?"

He flashed his smile. "I figured after living in Newark, Hell couldn't help but look good by comparison. Or at the least I'd be used to it."

"It's not that bad!"

"Have you ever tried living there?"

"I've never lived in Tahiti, either," Teresa pointed out. "But I think it'd be pretty nice."

"That's a good point," he said. He thought for a moment. "On the other hand, I've never lived in Chernobyl, but I've a fair idea I'd not like it much."

* * *

"Have you been to Baltimore?" she asked an hour later. They were getting close to that city.

"Oh, aye," James said. "A few years back, in the line of work."

"Tell me something about it."

He considered. "Well, I've heard the tale that when he'd been elected, Abe Lincoln was on his way to Washington to take his oath of office. Back in 1861, this would be. His train was set to go through Baltimore, but the good citizens were no great fans of his. The lad's bodyguards had some concerns that someone would try to put a bullet in him, and they were most likely right about that. So they sent the official train into the city as planned, but the clever lad had already passed through on another train, in disguise, and the would-be assassins had to go home, disappointed."

Teresa smiled. "Remind you of someone?"

"We're carrying on a fine tradition of subterfuge, you and I," he said. "I hope wherever old Abe is, he's right proud of us."

"But Lincoln was assassinated," she reminded him. "In the end."

He shrugged. "A lad's luck can't last forever. He'd a good run: saved his country, got his face on the penny and the five-dollar note, gave some fine speeches, and wound up with a grand statue in Washington. There's no point in getting greedy."

She wrapped her arms around herself. "We're not going to get away," she said quietly.

"Of course we are," James objected. "We're practically home free already. Those bastards who want to hurt you may have a great deal of pull in New York, but we're well away from that place. Most organizations of that sort haven't much reach outside their home turf."

"That's not what I meant," she said. "I'm talking about the long haul, not the getaway. When's the trial going to be? How many months? What happens after that? If I help send that young man away, he'll have friends who won't forget. I can't live on the run forever, James. But if I try to go home, someone will find out, and then they'll get me."

James looked away and drummed his fingers on the steering wheel. "I'll not let that happen," he said.

"You can't guard me forever."

Those words accomplished something Teresa hadn't known was possible. They shut James up completely, for a good long while. They rode in silence, each left alone with their own thoughts, until they passed Washington and angled west on I-66.

*   *   *

The flight attendant was taking drink orders. Teresa asked for a mineral water. Norma took ginger ale.

"With my Stanley, I always knew he wanted to marry me," Norma said. "It was written all over his face. Men really aren't very good at hiding their feelings. I imagine you knew what your James was thinking."

"I knew he liked me," Teresa said. "I would have to be blind not to see it. But I didn't know his intentions."

"Did you encourage him?" Norma asked.

Teresa smiled. "James is not a man who requires much encouragement."

"He's a man," Norma said. "I hope you didn't make it too easy on him—or too hard."

Chapter 4

They had lunch at a roadside diner just west of Washington. James's good nature, fortified by food, recovered quickly. He became more talkative again.

Teresa didn't. She was already feeling pangs of homesickness.

"Is your situation something you're not wanting to discuss?" he finally asked, after she'd failed to respond to several conversational gambits.

She sighed. "I shouldn't have listened to that detective."

"Erin can be right persuasive," James said with a grin. "I took her out dancing once."

"You dated her?" Teresa exclaimed, startled out of her funk.

"Oh aye, Erin and I go back a fair ways. That's one of the reasons I'm here now. She had to have someone she could trust."

"Are the two of you still seeing each other?"

James made a strange sound in his throat. "We're... friends," he said. "Naught more than that. But we've been through some difficult times together, and I'll warrant she knows what to expect of me."

"Are you a detective, too?"

"Nay," he laughed. "They'd hardly offer me a gold shield, love."

Teresa nodded. "James?"

"Aye?"

"You've seen a lot of crime scenes, haven't you?"

He smiled, as if he found something funny about what she'd said. "A few."

"Have you ever seen a dead body?"

"Aye. More than one."

"Have you ever seen anyone die?"

He wasn't smiling anymore. "Aye."

"I didn't actually see him kill that girl," she said softly. "I only saw him after, on the stairs. Bloody, with a knife in his hand, but I didn't see him stab her. Maybe that won't be good enough evidence. Maybe the jury won't convict him."

"That pretty boy Vitelli?" James snorted. "Nay, they've got him. You can put him at the scene, and that's one nail in his coffin, but they've others to hammer in. You needn't worry about Angel Face. He'll not be seeing the street again, at least not until his boyish good looks are a distant memory."

"You know him?" Teresa was surprised again.

"I've crossed his path once or twice," he said. "How was it you saw him?"

"I was on my way back from the store. I had bags of groceries in both hands, so I had to set a bag down on the landing to get out my keys. Isabella lived upstairs from me, in the same brownstone. I fished my keys out of my pocket, heard a noise, and there he was, coming down the stairs. We stared at each other for a second, and I could see him deciding whether to..."

"To kill you?" he asked gently.

She nodded. "I was frozen," she said. "I couldn't move, even to save my life, until he started walking again. Then I got inside, somehow, and bolted the door. He... he was standing on the landing. It seemed like a very long time, but in the end, he left. I don't think... I don't think he wanted to kill me."

"They don't like to kill civilians," James said. "It brings the wrong kind of attention. And these lads like to feel they've a code, that they're somehow the good guys. Or not the villains, at least."

"He changed his mind," Teresa said. "Later."

"Or someone changed it for him," James said. "His da, I'd imagine."

"Or I did, when I agreed to testify."

"That was brave, love."

"It was stupid."

"You know how to tell the difference between bravery and stupidity, don't you, love?"

"How?"

His eyes sparkled. "If it works, it was brave. If it doesn't, it was stupid."

"I don't feel brave," she said.

"Brave folks usually don't."

"Are you brave?"

He laughed. "Me? Perish the thought, love. Ask anyone who knows me. I'm neither brave nor stupid."

"So what are you?"

"I'm plain barking mad."

*   *   *

"So, love," James said, a few miles later. "I know you've no bairns of your own."

"How do you know that?" she replied.

"You'd hardly be going without them," he shot back. "A lass will leave her lover, aye. Her parents, too, but her wee ones? Perish the thought."

"You're right," she said. "I guess I'm just an old maid schoolteacher."

"Come, love, you're far too pretty to be a spinster," he laughed. "Surely you've a young man, at least, making eyes at you?"

She hesitated. "Not... not really," she admitted. "I was never that interested in boys." In truth, she didn't think she was all that pretty. She was too heavy for the American ideal, too old, too shy.

He glanced at her. "Are you meaning you weren't interested in them, or they weren't interested in you?"

"Maybe both."

James shook his head. "What you've to remember, love, is that lads are, on the whole, idiots. Particularly where women are concerned. Half of us don't know what we want, even when it's right in front of us, and the other half are usually making the wrong choices."

She couldn't help but laugh at that. "Which one are you?"

"You're persisting in putting me in a box," he said.

"You're the one who keeps splitting people up into two categories," she retorted. "Are you afraid to commit yourself?"

"You're hardly the first lass to accuse me of that," he chuckled. "In this case, it's an easy question. I'm the one making bad decisions."

"Is that why you're here?"

He threw her a startled look. "What makes you say a thing like that?" The car drifted over the center line.

"Eyes on the road," she reminded him.

"Oh, I know where we're going," he said absently. "Well enough to get there."

"Is this one of your bad decisions?" she persisted.

James shook his head. "Nay, love, I think it's one of my better ones."

"Why?"

"I don't know." He was watching the road, a slight smile quirking one corner of his mouth. "It's just a feeling."

"Are you married, James?" The question just slipped out, no planning.

He looked startled again. "Me? Nay, lass, not even the once."

"Why not?" She couldn't resist tweaking him just a little, mimicking his accent. "Surely you've a young lass, at least, making eyes at you?"

He laughed. "More than one, come to that."

"But never the right one?"

"All of them seem like the right one at the time," he said.

"But not in the morning?"

He shot her another look. "Now, love, just what are you accusing me of? I don't leave a lass who wants me to stay."

"So none of them want you to stay?"

He didn't answer.

"That's hard to believe," Teresa said under her breath.

"Teresa, love," James said, "I've only just met you, so I've no idea when you're telling the truth, and when you're just winding me up."

"James," she answered, "I think that's the first time you've said my name."

"I suppose you're right," he said after a moment. "I got it right, aye? Teresa Tommasino?"

"That's me. And you're James."

"James Corcoran. You can always call me Corky, or even Corks. Most everyone does."

"I'm not most everyone."

"I can see that," he said. "I'm starting to think you're someone special, love."

*   *   *

The route James had chosen took them down Interstate 81. It was beautiful country, the road tracing the line of the Appalachians between the Shenandoah National Park and the George Washington and Jefferson National Forest, probably the most awkwardly-named piece of woods in America. For Teresa, who'd rarely been out of Brooklyn, the landscape was amazing.

"I can't decide," she said, staring away west toward the setting sun and squinting against the glare. "Half the time I feel like I'm running for my life. The other half, I feel like I'm on vacation."

He laughed. "I'm flattered in either case."

"Why's that?"

"On the one hand, I've a lass looking to me for protection. On the other, I've a fair colleen choosing to share my company for a good long while. I can't lose."

"I see. Where are we going to spend the night?"

"I'm thinking we can make Roanoke. But there's no particular hurry."

"There isn't someplace we need to be? For the plan?"

"I've told you, love. The whole point of this arrangement is that no one knows where we are. In point of fact, wandering the nation's highways might be the safest place you could be. Admit it, the prospect's not without attraction."

"It feels a little strange," she said, realizing that she really was completely at the mercy of this unusual Irishman. It was scary, but he was right; there was a thrill to it. The thought came to Teresa that, as far as the world was concerned, she was dead. She had no obligations at all. The school superintendent wouldn't be expecting her to turn up for work. She had no schedule, no commitments. In a way, it was like being born all over again. She took a slow, deep breath. Her lungs seemed to expand further than they ever had. Or maybe it was the tightness she'd been carrying in her chest since seeing Angel Face Vitelli loosening just a little.

"That's better, love," James said approvingly.

"What do you mean?"

"That extra bit of anxiety you've been carrying around with you, it's been putting some strain on the suspension of this fine automobile."

"Are you saying something about my weight, Mr. Corcoran?" she demanded with mock severity.

He put up a hand. "Nay, I've no objection to your shape at all. It's rather fine, in fact."

She felt herself blush, remembering her pajamas, or lack thereof, and the appreciative way he'd looked at her legs. She looked out the window again and stopped talking.

*   *   *

James steered the Accord into the parking lot of the La Quinta Inn on the edge of Roanoke a little after dark. They'd stopped for dinner at a Mexican grill nearby, on his suggestion that it would be a good idea to acclimate themselves to the cuisine, as long as they were heading for the border. Teresa had offered to take a turn driving, but under questioning, had been forced to admit she didn't own a car and had hardly driven the past decade. James had kept driving.

Despite the long hours behind the wheel, he was as bright and cheery as he'd been when they'd started. His energy seemed inexhaustible, and she wondered whether anything could possibly dampen his spirits.

"Don't you ever get tired?" she asked as they entered the lobby.

He grinned. "I'll have plenty of time for sleeping. But when I'm awake, I'm awake."

James paid cash for the room, peeling more bills off his roll. He gave their names as Mr. and Mrs. O'Brien.

"So, we're married now?" she asked as they rode the elevator up to the third floor.

"Lass," he said, "if you think all the couples who check into hotels as husband and wife are lawfully wed, you've led an even more sheltered life than I thought."

"I suppose it avoids attention," she said thoughtfully. "Even in the twenty-first century. But what about when the maid finds both beds slept in?"

"Now you're thinking tactical thoughts," he said approvingly. "And it's a good question. But it needn't concern us. They'll merely think we're on the outs."

"Or maybe you snore," she offered with a giggle.

"Or perhaps you've terribly cold feet," he suggested.

"Or you toss and turn."

"Or perhaps we used both beds," he said with a sly smile. "First the one, then the other."

It took her a second to understand his meaning. Then she went red all the way to the tips of her ears. "James!"

"You're particularly pretty when you're taken aback," he said. "You're lovelier than you think you are. When you forget yourself and let yourself be happy, it shines through."

While she was still thinking how to take what he'd said, the elevator arrived at their floor. She busied herself with the room key and avoided eye contact.

It was only once they'd settled in that she remembered what she'd forgotten. She'd been meaning to ask to stop at a clothing store and pick up some sleep pants, but somehow, it had slipped her mind. Besides, there'd been a definite absence of shopping malls along their route. But one more night wouldn't do any harm. James had been a perfect gentleman so far. And, Teresa reminded herself, she really had no choice but to trust him.

James might be full of energy, but Teresa was exhausted. Her body felt like it knew all about the hundreds of miles they'd put behind them. She showered, brushed her teeth, and came out of the bathroom in her long T-shirt with less self-consciousness than the night before. James was sitting on the far bed, propped against the headboard, twirling something in his fingers. He glanced up and once more she was aware of his attention, of the warmth in his bright green eyes as he looked her up and down.

"Comfortable?" he asked.

"Yes. What's that in your hand?"

"Oh, this? It's nothing." He flicked his wrist and the thing was gone.

She put her hands on her hips and gave him her best schoolteacher stare. "Come on. Show me."

He raised his eyebrows, but produced the item out of his right sleeve. She approached and looked down at it.

"What is that?" she asked again. It looked like a molded handle of some sort, but a handle that wasn't attached to anything.

He pressed something on it and flicked his wrist. There was a smooth, metallic sound, and Teresa jumped back as a four-inch blade of shining steel sprang out.

"My goodness," she said weakly.

"It's a Scarab tactical knife," James said, sliding the blade carefully back into its resting place. "Just a bit of personal insurance. I feel better having it about me."

"Do many cops carry... tactical knives?"

"Not many coppers I know of," he said. "But you'd be surprised how handy these can be. This sort of knife saved my life not so long ago."

"Oh my God," she said, putting a hand up to her face. "You stabbed someone?"

"Nothing like that," he said with a smile. "I lent it to a mutual friend to deactivate a dangerous device I happened to be holding."

"A mutual friend?"

"Ah, that'd be Erin O'Reilly."

"She saved your life?"

"Aye. So we're in good company, you and I. You might say I owe her a favor."

"And that's why you're here, doing this?"

"It's one reason."

"And the others?"

"Well, I didn't know you at the time," he said with a knowing twinkle in his eye. "But now that I do, a bit, other reasons have occurred to me."

"You like making me uncomfortable," she said.

"I do like getting your attention."

She shook her head. "Good night, James."

"Sleep tight, love. I'll be here when you wake."

*   *   *

The car exploded. The wave of heat and noise rolled over Teresa. This time, the flames were closer. She saw her hair smoldering, felt the terrible, scorching flames. Pieces of jagged metal rained down. With terrible clarity, she saw a hand and arm, an arm attached to nothing, sailing through the air.

She woke up with a gasp, a scream locked in her throat, trembling violently. She was cold and overheated at the same time, unsure where she was or what was happening.

Someone was holding her from behind, strong arms wrapped around her. A warm body was pressed close against her. Still disoriented, she instinctively moved closer to that comforting warmth.

"Hush, love," a voice said in her ear. "It's all right. No need to fret, I'm here. I've got you."

"James?" she said hesitantly, her memories finally catching up to her.

"Would you be expecting someone else?"

Now she was fully awake and aware. She was lying in bed, and James was right there with her. The only things between their bodies were her T-shirt and underwear, and his boxer shorts. She hesitated, torn between a sudden rush of modesty and the residual fear of her nightmare.

He felt the tension in her body. "Easy, love," he whispered. "Easy. I'll not harm you." His hands were gentle, resting just above her hips.

"What are you doing?" she asked in a low voice.

"You cried out in your sleep," he said. "You were thrashing about. I'd an idea you'd appreciate a bit of reassurance."

That might be true, but she felt something else in him, a sort of veiled, coiled energy. It sent a thrill almost of fear through her. "What do you want?" she whispered.

"Love, I think we both know that," he said softly. His hand moved lower, onto the curve of her hip. "But I'm not wanting anything you're not willing to give."

She shivered again, without even knowing why. Feelings she didn't know or understand were running through her veins. Her entire body felt sensitive, tingling at every touch. She could hardly bear the contact with him, but she wanted more.

"James..." she began, not knowing whether she was going to ask him to go away or to hold her tighter.

His lips brushed her cheek, just in front of her ear. She started in surprise, then made a soft sound. She unconsciously arched her back against him.

James's hand moved to her shoulder, turning her over to face him. She stared into his eyes in the near-dark of the hotel room, seeing something deep and wild and indescribable in them. She felt his breath against her face. Her own lips parted. She stared back, pleading with her eyes.

He held the moment, letting it stretch out for what felt like long minutes. Then something she could neither see nor hear broke the tension. He smiled down at her, his usual charming self again.

"You're all right now, lass," he said. "Try to get some more sleep. We've a long road before us. I'll be right here if you're needing me." Then, to her surprise, he lay down beside her and closed his eyes.

Teresa lay on her back, looking up at the ceiling, feeling strangely let down. She didn't know what surprised her more—that she'd been disappointed he'd stopped when he had, or at the look she'd seen in James's eyes just before he pulled away. He hadn't meant to withdraw. He'd meant to do... something. She couldn't shake the thought that he'd been surprised at his own reluctance. Because Teresa knew, in a part of herself she didn't want to admit to, that if he'd tried to take things further, to take *her*, she probably would have let him, might even have welcomed it.

* * *

Norma sipped her ginger ale. "So, if this young man pursued you, why are you apart now?"

"*Pardon?*" *Teresa asked.*

"*You said he lived in New York. If he was so keen on you, why is he there, and you were in San Diego?*"

Teresa smiled, a little sadly. "*There were complications. We did not wish to be parted.*"

"*Long distance relationships are hard,*" *Norma said, nodding sympathetically.* "*Will he be meeting you at the airport? I don't mind telling you, I'd like to take a look at this fine fellow, after all you've told me.*"

"*No. He... does not know I am coming.*"

"*A surprise visit!*" *Norma was delighted.* "*He'll be so happy to see you, dear!*"

"*I hope so,*" *Teresa said. She looked at the mineral water in her hand, remembering Glen Docherty-Kinlochewe whiskey from James's hip flask, and tequila with orange juice and grenadine. She hoped he wouldn't be angry with her for coming. She hoped he wanted to see her. But mostly, she hoped he was still alive.*

Chapter 5

The further from New York they got, the safer Teresa felt. Everything that had happened—the murder, the police, the bomb blast—got smaller in their rear-view mirror. With every day, she felt better around James. She knew he wanted her; he'd made no secret of it. But he didn't make any further moves. He was just as talkative as before, but he wasn't trying to win her over. At least, not that way. They slept in separate beds, and he didn't touch her anywhere inappropriate. But James Corcoran was a man who liked physical contact. When he touched her hand, or her arm, she could still feel the desire pulsing in his blood.

Knowing James wanted her but was holding back would have frightened the old Teresa. But the new Teresa who was slowly emerging on this strange road trip found it exhilarating. She felt more daring than before, like his desire gave her a power over the man. She found herself initiating contact, reaching out for him, not even worrying about the consequences. He kept being friendly and warm, holding himself in check, which only emboldened her more. It was probably dangerous, she told herself, but she didn't stop.

They left Virginia and passed through Knoxville, then headed across Tennessee by way of Chattanooga, on into Alabama. The weather was warm, the air thick and sticky. James told stories he'd heard from Teamsters about long-haul truck rides through the Deep South. One of the advantages of working in the shipping business was that he knew men who'd been to every state in the Union. His store of anecdotes was bottomless, most of them funny, a few sweet, some scary, but always told in a way that made her smile at the end.

Their fifth day on the road, they landed at a Holiday Inn near Jackson, Mississippi. They checked in, paying cash, as always, and giving the name Callahan. James helped carry their luggage up to the room and started rummaging through their travel bags, piling up clothing on the bed nearest the door.

"I'm stepping out for a bit," he said.

"Okay," Teresa said. "Should I come with you?"

"Nay, I'll not be long. Is there anything you're needing?"

She picked up the notepad next to the phone, thought for a moment, and scribbled down a few basic cosmetics and personal items.

He took the list and nodded. "I should be able to get these. Oh, one other thing. I'll be needing your clothes."

"I beg your pardon?"

He pointed at her and grinned. "Those clothes, love. Your underthings, too."

"James!"

His grin didn't falter. "Didn't you see the Laundromat on the way in? Unless you'd like to be wearing dirty things all the way to Mexico?"

"What am I supposed to wear in the meantime?" But she couldn't hide a slight smile of her own.

He eyed her appreciatively. "That's your decision, love. I'll keep my opinions to myself."

Teresa stood up and walked into the bathroom. She felt an impish, teasing desire to put him off balance a little, to pay him back for all the times he'd made her uncomfortable. As she went, she very deliberately and slowly unbuttoned the first two buttons of her blouse.

It worked better than she'd expected. James licked his lips and actually seemed a little nervous. It was only for a second, and he recovered fast, but she'd seen the momentary weakness. It felt good.

She closed the bathroom door and undressed. Seeing the bathtub, she decided to kill two birds with one stone and started the hot water running. Then she bundled her clothes up, opened the door a few inches, and dropped the dirty clothes outside.

"Don't get lost, James," she called and shut the door again. She considered locking it, then decided not to. Knowing he could just turn the knob and walk right in was deliciously exciting to consider, theoretically. If he actually did, she'd probably have a heart attack.

Wondering at her own state of mind, thinking what her mother would say to her, Teresa lowered herself into the bath. She lay back and let the heat sink into her flesh, closing her eyes. What she saw in her mind was James Corcoran's face. She thought back to that night when she'd woken from her nightmare to find herself in his arms. She tried to imagine the feel of his lips, wondering what it would be like to kiss him. Would he be gentle? Passionate? Demanding? She didn't know. Possibilities chased themselves through her head. She hoped he'd get back soon, though she didn't know what would happen when he got there. Probably nothing. It was all just a game in their minds, wasn't it?

*   *   *

The click of the lock on the main door jolted her awake. She sat up with a splash, lukewarm water slopping over the rim of the tub. She hadn't meant to fall asleep, and for a wild, disorienting instant, she had no idea where she was. Then she heard James's voice.

"Teresa, love. Everything all right?"

"Yes," she called. She stood up and reached for a towel. "I'll be out in a minute."

"Grand. I've all manner of things here. Food, drink, fresh clothes, everything a lass desires."

Teresa dried herself quickly and wrapped the towel around her. She took another towel and bundled her hair into it. She glanced at herself in the mirror. The terrycloth covered the important areas, but she was showing an awful lot of leg.

She opened the bathroom door a couple of inches. "James?"

There he was, smiling cheerfully, just on the other side of the door. "Aye?"

"Can you hand me some clothes, please?"

His eyes drifted down from her face, taking in the strategically-placed towel. "Fair enough," he said. He took out a T-shirt, jeans, and a pair of underwear and handed them through the gap. A deliciously familiar smell drifted in along with the clothing.

"James! You went to an Italian restaurant!"

He grinned. "I found a place that was willing to make something to go. I'm afraid I've no good sense what kind of pasta you like, but I reckoned spaghetti was safe enough. I thought you'd appreciate a wee taste of home."

To Teresa's surprise, her eyes blurred with sudden tears. "That's... that's very kind of you, James," she said. Then she closed the door and leaned her back against it. She'd been overwhelmed for a moment with memories. But home was hundreds of miles away. How long would it be before she tasted her mother's cooking again? Had they held a funeral for her? They would have needed a closed-casket service. The body that had served as her decoy would be in no condition to be viewed. She shuddered.

She started to get dressed, realizing only then that she didn't have a bra and the T-shirt James had given her was white, and fairly thin fabric. She considered asking him for some more clothes, then decided not to call attention to it. She buttoned her jeans, pulled the shirt over her head, and walked out, barefoot, wet-haired, projecting a confidence she almost felt.

The overhead lights were off. To her surprise, she saw a pair of candles glimmering in the dimness. James had laid out their dinner on the table by the window. The plates were paper, the silverware and cups plastic, but the pasta smelled wonderful. He stood up and pulled back her chair, an old-school gentleman's gesture.

"Stag's Leap cabernet," he said, uncorking the wine. "A bit too good for disposable cups, but a fine sight better than something out of a box." He poured a little into her glass and looked at her expectantly.

Teresa knew what to do. She picked up the glass and held it under her nose, letting the bouquet find its way into her nostrils. Then she took a small sip. She wasn't much of a drinker, except at family gatherings, and the wine there was twenty dollars a bottle. She didn't know wine, but she could still taste the difference. This was a good, expensive wine.

Licking her lips, she nodded. "That's very good," she said.

"Better or worse than Glen D?" he asked with a twinkle in his eye as he filled her glass.

"Different," she said. "That's like asking whether a painting is better than a concert."

James grinned. "That's right poetic of you, love." He picked up his own glass. "Here's to us."

Teresa twirled the strands of spaghetti around her fork and took a bite.

She'd known that music, sounds, and smells could carry her mind back to old memories and experiences. Now she learned flavor could do the same thing. She closed her eyes and let the blend of Italian spices carry her back to New York, to a time when she hadn't been afraid or hurting.

When she opened her eyes again, James was staring into her face across the table. His eyes were filled with softness, tenderness, and a kind of wonder.

"What?" she asked, self-consciousness making her glance down at her plate.

"The face of a lass who's forgotten herself, caught up in the experience, is one of the loveliest things a lad can see," he said. "I'm enjoying the moment, just as you are."

"James, this is just food," she said, feeling herself blush.

"What difference does that make?"

She didn't have an answer to that. "You're being very nice to me," she said instead. "You're coming on to me, aren't you?"

"Do you want me to?"

She looked up again, against her better judgment. A dozen negatives died behind her lips, but she couldn't make herself say yes, either. She hit him with one of his own weapons, answering a question with a question. "Do you want to?"

"It'd be easier," he said, and now it was his turn to look away.

"Easier than what?"

He didn't answer, pretending to busy himself with his food. She reached across the table and put a hand on his. She felt a slight tremble in his fingers, those hands that were so sure and steady.

"James?"

He looked back at her and smiled with a hint of sadness. "I've a job to do here, love. To see no harm comes to you. My best mate in the world asked me to, and I'd do anything for him. Added to that, I'm paying back another friend. And she did say I oughtn't get too close to you. But now..."

She squeezed his hand. "What now?"

"Now I'm getting to know you a bit, and I find I don't care what anyone told me to do. I'd take care of you no matter what."

"Of course you would," she said. "I mean, that's your job."

"This isn't about my job," he said quickly. "Look, love, forget I said anything. What's important is you're happy and safe. How do you like your dinner?"

"You were watching me eat it," she said, smiling. "How do you think I liked it?"

"Words fail me."

She laughed. "Not likely."

"They say I've a silver tongue," he agreed. "But I'd need one of solid gold to describe you."

"I'm not that pretty, James. Surely you've met more beautiful girls."

"I have," he agreed, and he looked a little confused. "Look, Teresa, I'm not a particularly good man."

"Nonsense."

"I mean it. I've done many a thing I'm not proud of. But the way you look at me, the way you talk to me, the way you trust me... You do trust me, don't you?"

"Of course I do," she said. "I'm here, aren't I? You're the only man on Earth who knows where I am right now. My life... My whole life's in your hands." She had trouble getting the last words out.

"Aye," he said softly. "Maybe that's it."

Their hands were still touching. His fingers curled around hers. They weren't trembling any longer. He stood up from the table, without letting go of her hand. She turned in her chair. He went down on one knee in front of her. The candlelight shone reflected in his bright green eyes. Teresa was very conscious of his nearness, the touch of his hand on hers.

"James," she whispered. "What are you..."

Then he leaned in and kissed her.

Teresa hadn't been kissed in a very long time. The feeling was both strange and familiar. The warm pressure of his lips against hers was almost overwhelming. She was reflexively pulling away at the moment of contact, but at his touch, she instinctively moved toward him again. Her back arched and her lips opened slightly. She tasted James Corcoran, the wine and tomato sauce from supper, a hint of saltiness on his mouth, and an underlying, undefinable sweetness. He drew the breath out of her lungs. Dimly, she was aware of his hand entwined with her fingers and of his other hand cupping her cheek.

He drew away. She opened her eyes with a faint gasp. He was looking at her, their faces only inches apart.

Teresa licked her lips and shivered, but not from cold. "James," she began again. "I—"

"Aye?" He leaned slightly closer.

She trailed into silence, closing her eyes in anticipation. For what felt like long, endless seconds, she wondered if she had misinterpreted his intentions. Then she felt the faint brush of his lips, so light it was like the trailing edge of a dream. He danced away from her touch and she chased him, seeking him out. He let her catch him, capturing her in return. As the kiss deepened, Teresa's whole body came alive. She tingled all over, delicious heat kindling in her belly. Phantom fingers seemed to be tracing her skin. She was very aware of the thin cotton of her shirt rubbing against her flesh.

Then she realized some of the touch was James's fingertips. His hand slid up her side and caressed her breast through her shirt. She groaned quietly and felt herself press against his hand. It was heavenly, intoxicating, maddening. The tip of his tongue flicked teasingly against her lips. She opened her mouth wider. Her veins were swollen with liquid fire, melting her from the inside.

James's lips moved away from hers to her cheek, down to her neck. He kissed and nuzzled the hollow of her throat. She leaned back in her chair and put her hands up to his shoulders.

"Oh, God," she murmured. "James, what are you doing to me?"

He paused. "Does it please you, love?"

"Yes. No. I don't know."

"Shall I stop?"

"I don't know."

He chuckled, the sound vibrating deliciously where his lips pressed against her. One of his hands eased up under her shirt, caressing the sensitive skin just below her belly. She trembled, but whether from sensation or anticipation, she couldn't have said. She felt simultaneously separated from her body and at the same time more attuned to it than ever before. As if in a dream, she felt his fingertips trace the lines of her body, moving higher, lifting her shirt, trailing along her ribcage. He kissed her again, deeply.

Then he pulled away. Teresa stared at him, breathing hard. He stared back, and to her astonishment, he looked almost frightened. His eyes were shining. Without thinking, she reached out and touched his cheek. His skin was warm to the touch. His hand went up to hers. Holding her, he turned and gently kissed her wrist, then her palm. She shivered again. His mouth opened wider and he slowly closed his lips around the tip of her index finger. His tongue pressed against her finger.

The intimacy of that gesture, so unexpected, made her eyes widen.

He stood up and drew her with him. Her legs were weak and wobbly, but she obediently followed his lead. At that moment, she would have followed him anywhere. He backed her against the edge of the bed. She half sat, half fell. Moving with his easy, unbelievable speed, his hand was already behind her head before it could strike the bed. Then he was above her, their bodies pressed together, one of his legs coming up between her thighs, and he was kissing her again and again. Every moment, every touch brought her closer to something both familiar and unknown.

His fingers were working nimbly at her waist, unbuttoning her jeans. Teresa felt just a little fear under the building excitement.

He felt her momentary hesitation. "Are you all right, love?" he murmured.

"James? I... be careful with me," she stammered.

"I'll not hurt you. Never."

"I mean, it's just... I haven't... I mean..."

He raised himself away from her to arm's length and considered her. "This is something you've not done before?"

Teresa was ashamed of herself now, of her inexperience. She shook her head silently.

He looked at her for what seemed a very long time. The shame built up in her. She should have pretended she knew more about men, should have just gone with the feeling. She'd ruined the moment, maybe ruined everything.

"I'm sorry," she said. If she hadn't been trapped beneath him, she would have turned away.

"Sorry?" he echoed, astonished. "Teresa, you've nothing to apologize for. No, it's me should be apologizing. I should have realized. It's such a rare thing these days."

"Is it... a problem?"

"It's something we should talk about, I'm thinking," he said. He licked his lips and cleared his throat. "And the rest of our dinner's getting cold." He levered himself to his feet and offered his hand to help her up.

She took his hand, feeling very strange; a blend of lightheaded exhilaration and embarrassment. She ran a hand through her hair, still damp from her bath and now very tangled. She straightened her shirt and sat down at the table once more.

They ate for a few moments in silence. It was hard for Teresa to look at him.

"James?" she ventured at last, cautiously.

"Aye?"

"Do you still... like me?"

He smiled. "Very much, love. And it was a very near thing between finishing this excellent pasta, and stripping the clothes from your lovely body and having my wicked way with you."

"James!"

His smile widened. "Is it any wonder lads get confused? Lasses tell us they want honesty, then they act shocked when we say what's on our minds."

"I'm the one who's confused," she said. "If that's how you feel, why did you stop?"

James looked rueful now. "I'll admit to being somewhat more experienced than you in this sort of thing," he said. "You're special, Teresa. I don't want this to simply be something we do on the road, keeping one another company. You deserve better than me."

Teresa stared. He couldn't possibly mean that, but she saw nothing but plain honesty in his eyes. "You're a fine man, James," she said. "Any woman would be lucky to have you."

"I'll not be at your side forever," he said quietly. "What about once the job's done? Once Angel Face is safely locked up and you're free from danger?"

"What are you saying?"

"I'm a rare one to be thinking of the future at a time like this," he said. "But I said I'd not harm you, and I meant it. That includes breaking your heart."

She tried a smile of her own. "Someone's got quite a high opinion of himself," she said.

His grin returned, like the sun poking through the clouds. "You're saying you'd not be brokenhearted if I left you alone and forlorn?"

"I got through my first three decades without you. I survived somehow."

"Ah, but you didn't know I was out there then."

"What if you're the one whose heart breaks?" she shot back.

"Have you never broken a lad's heart before?"

"Not that I know of."

"Well, my heart's never been broken," he said. "So if that does happen, we'll both learn something new. Would you care for more wine? We've a bit left in the bottle."

"Okay," she said, holding out her cup. They drained the last of the wine.

James got up to clear the table. "What I love about meals on the road," he commented. "No dishes to wash." He swept the remains of the meal into the garbage can. "Now, we've a good few miles still in front of us. Perhaps we'd best be getting to bed."

She stood up. "James?"

"Aye?"

"Has anyone ever told you, you sometimes talk too much?"

"Constantly."

"It's funny," she said. "Most people, when they talk, want to share their feelings. But I think you use words to distract people, so they don't know what you're feeling."

"I'm an open book, love," he said. "Heart on my sleeve."

"Is that so?"

"Ask me anything."

"Have you ever been in love?"

"I'm thinking of a story you might like. This would be back in the late '80s, when I was serving with the Brigades. We'd just done a bank job, a fundraising sort of thing, you understand. A few of the lads and I were holed up in a flat just down the road from the bank..."

Teresa smiled. "I rest my case."

He returned the smile. "I may not answer all your questions, but I'll not lie to you, love."

She stepped closer to him. If she didn't figure out one thing, she'd be awake half the night wondering. He'd come right to the edge of his self-control, but he'd held back from making love to her. The question was, did he still want her, now that the moment had passed? She could ask him, or she could find out.

The new Teresa Tommasino, the daring adventuress, slipped her arms around his waist and pressed her body against his. She tilted her head and kissed him. She felt his desire, as clear and plain as anything.

Feeling like a terrible tease, she released him. "Goodnight, James," she said. She couldn't resist adding, "Pleasant dreams."

He laughed quietly. "That's a safe wager. Goodnight, Teresa."

*   *   *

"You shouldn't worry about him, dear," Norma said.

"What do you mean?" Teresa asked.

"Something's the matter. When you talk about your young man, I see little worry lines on your forehead. Are you worried he won't be happy to see you?"

"Oh, no. Not at all. But..."

"But?"

Teresa sighed. "There was... an incident. He's in the hospital. That's why I'm going to New York."

Norma put a hand to her mouth. "Oh, you poor dear! How terrible! I had no idea. Is he going to be all right?"

"I don't know."

"No wonder you're worried, poor thing." Norma patted Teresa's hand. "What can this nosy old woman do to help?"

"You just met me," Teresa said. "You don't have to do anything."

"You know which hospital he's in, I'm sure," Norma said.

Teresa nodded.

"Do you know how you're getting there?"

"I'll get a taxi."

"No, you won't," Norma said in decisive tones. "My grandson is picking me up at the airport. We'll take you to the hospital."

"I couldn't possibly ask you to do that."

"You didn't ask, dear. I offered. If we don't help each other, what does that say about us?"

"I don't know how to thank you, Mrs. Malecek."

"Dear, we're well past that. It's Norma. And you can thank me by taking good care of your man."

"He does need looking after. Trouble seems to have a way of finding him."

Chapter 6

James had said they should talk about it, but he didn't say anything about their encounter the following morning. He was as pleasantly talkative as ever, still full of amusing anecdotes. They drove south on Interstate 55 from Jackson, down into Louisiana. James told stories about New Orleans. Apparently he knew several Irish longshoremen in that city, and had been there on a particularly interesting Mardi Gras.

"I assure you, everything you've heard about that holiday is true," he said. "Particularly on Bourbon Street. I came back with a good collection of bead necklaces."

Teresa hadn't actually heard many stories about Mardi Gras. "How do you get those?" she asked.

James glanced sidelong at her, surprised. "There's a bit of a tradition about them," he said. "During the parade, just before the start of Lent, the lads on the floats toss beads to the crowd. You just need to get their attention."

"And how do you do that?"

"Well, if you're a lass, it's easy enough."

"Show them a pretty face?" she suggested.

He nodded. "Aye. Except it's not precisely your face you'd be showing them."

She didn't get it. Then she did, and felt the blood rush to her cheeks. "I see."

"Just so."

"But I'm confused," she said. "If women get beads by... showing off, then how did you end up with so many? You don't have those parts."

"That's a fine question," he said. "I'd had rather a lot to drink that evening. I woke up in a hotel I didn't know, on the far side of town, with five necklaces and a bad headache. I couldn't exactly tell you how I came by them. Except the headache, of course."

"You've been all over the place," she said. "Every mile we drive, it's the furthest I've been from home, but you always know the territory. Are we going through New Orleans?"

"Nay, that's a dead end," he said. "We'd have to hop a boat to Mexico, and I get a mite queasy on the open sea. Besides, Vitelli has contacts down in the Big Easy. There's been Mafia all over that place ever since it was a mangrove swamp. Irish, too, but it's the Italians we'd be worrying about."

She shuddered. "But no one would be looking for me there. Would they?"

"Of course not," he agreed. "No one's looking for you at all, what with you being dead and all. But there's a long-shot chance someone might recognize me, and that could lead to trouble."

"Did you arrest some of them?"

"I'd a bit of a run-in with some Italians down this way a few years back. It's been a while, but those lads have long memories. Nay, we'll turn west before we get to Lake Ponchartrain and make for Baton Rouge."

"That sounds good."

"Not that you wouldn't do fine in New Orleans," he added.

"I'm sure I would."

"You'd get lots of beads."

"I don't doubt it," she said dryly.

* * *

"James?" she asked a few miles later.

"Aye?"

"How long are you going to stay with me?"

"I'll need to make sure you're safe," he said. "And I'll get you well settled and comfortable. But mostly it depends on you."

"On me?"

"On how long you're needing me there."

Teresa nodded and didn't reply. She was thinking about finding a place in a new city, knowing no one, constantly on the lookout for criminals and assassins. But she found that wasn't what she was really afraid of now. She was afraid of being alone. And she was afraid of having to say goodbye to James Corcoran.

"What if I wanted you to stay?" she asked.

"I can hang about a bit," he said.

"I mean, for a longer time," she said. "What would you say if I wanted you to stay... not for the job? For... me?"

He thought about his answer, which made her nervous. He was usually quick to respond.

"I'd say you're hitching your wagon to the wrong horse," he said at last. "Don't count on me, Teresa."

"That's a funny thing to say, when you're my bodyguard," she said. "If I can't trust you, what are we doing here?"

"That's not what I mean," he said. "I'll protect you, no fear. But I'm not the lad to build your future around."

That silenced her for the rest of the drive to Baton Rouge. They got there a little before lunchtime. They'd driven under the

    Tequila Sunrise

leading edge of a heavy cloud. Rain was falling by the time they entered the city limits.

"Have you ever eaten Cajun, love?" James asked.

"No."

"You've got to try it, at least the once. I knew a place, just across the river. Let's see if it's still open. You're not given to heartburn, I hope?"

"Not that I know of."

"If Creole cooking doesn't give it to you, nothing will," he said with a grin.

They drove through Baton Rouge to the Mississippi. As the car rolled across the bridge, James gave her a wink.

"Congratulations, love. You've just entered the West. The grand American frontier."

"I tell my students the frontier isn't there anymore," she said.

"Oh?" James looked startled. "What's happened to California, then? Don't tell me it's sunk into the ocean." He paused. "Not that it'd be any great loss if it has..."

They entered Port Allen, a suburb on the west side of the city. James clearly knew where he was going. Without hesitation or uncertainty, he steered them into the parking lot of a diner. "It's a casual spot," he explained. "Just right for folk on the road. I'm keen on the pork myself, but you're welcome to whatever you're wanting."

"That reminds me," she said as he parked. "What sort of expense account are you on?"

"I'll not be running short, if that's your worry."

They scrambled across the parking lot, dodging raindrops. The lot was mostly full and the lunchtime crowd made for a sizable line. They took their place at the end and Teresa squinted at the menu.

"You didn't answer my question," she said.

"Why are you worried?" he replied.

"I'm not," she said. "I'm curious. Are you spending your own money on me?"

"What if I was?"

"It'd be inappropriate."

He nodded and rubbed his chin, his face serious. "As opposed to some of the things we've been doing?"

"James!" she hissed, looking around. None of the other people in line were paying them any attention, but she was still embarrassed. "You have absolutely no shame!"

"None," he agreed cheerfully. "I find life's much more enjoyable without it."

When they got to the counter, James ordered a barbecued pork sandwich with coleslaw. Teresa, operating on the assumption that the man who'd been there before knew what he was doing, got the same. They picked up their food and found a table along the wall.

"This is serious," she said. "You can't treat this whole thing like... like some sort of game!"

He swallowed a bite of his sandwich and shrugged. "If you can't take serious things lightly, love, you'll waste half your life worrying."

She frowned at him. "I don't know what to make of you, James. One moment you're in control, taking care of everything. The next, you're nothing more than an overgrown kid. Then you're trying to... to seduce me. What am I supposed to think?"

He gave her another of his incandescent smiles, and despite her annoyance, it made her a little weak. "I'm with you in this, Terry. All the way in, all my chips on the table. I'll see you safe, no matter what. I hope it won't come to it, but should the situation require it, I'll shed blood for you. Mine or any other lad's, though I'd prefer holding on to my own. But in the meantime, I'm going to be me."

"You're not keeping your receipts," she said.

He blinked. "I'm sorry?"

Teresa shook her head. "You're not on an expense account. You throw your receipts away. You're not going to turn any of your expenses in. James, this trip must be costing a fortune!"

"You needn't trouble yourself on my account," he said. "So far as the money goes, I'm spending a certain amount from my own pocket. Does that bother you?"

She dropped her voice, despite the hubbub around them. "But won't the police want to know about... all this?"

He started to answer, then paused. The smile froze on his face. He was looking over her shoulder at something behind her. Teresa started to turn.

"Don't look," he said quietly. He was still smiling with his mouth, but not with his eyes. "Take that last bite of your meal."

Mystified by the sudden change in him, not quite frightened yet, she obeyed.

"We're going out the side door," he said. "This minute. I'll be right behind you. Walk fast, don't run. And don't look back."

"What's happening?" she asked, forcing herself not to turn her head. It was hard. The hairs on the back of her neck crackled like live electric wires.

"I'll explain later," he said. "If anything happens to me, don't try to help me. Run like your life depends on it. Stay in public, get to a police station. Don't be alone with anyone, not even if he's wearing a uniform, no matter what. You understand?"

"No," she whispered. All her fears crowded back on her. The sweet-sour tang of barbecue sauce churned in her stomach. But she kept walking through the lunchtime crowd of oblivious diners. She pushed the exit bar and opened the door. After the close confines of the restaurant, the humid, rainy Louisiana air felt clammy on her skin.

"You're doing grand, love," James said behind her. "Everything's going to be fine. Keep walking. Don't run, not till I say."

Their car seemed very far away, her feet moving slowly, like in a quicksand nightmare. But the distance gradually shrank until, after what felt like long minutes of struggle, she was able to put her hand on the passenger door. James slid into the driver's seat. Before she'd had time to fasten her seatbelt, the car was moving.

"What did you see?" she demanded as they left the parking lot, heading south.

"It might mean nothing," James said, but his eyes were on his rearview mirror. "I recognized a lad."

Teresa went very cold inside. "A gangster?"

"Aye. A fellow I met a few years back, name of Andreotti. Mafia foot-soldier. I'd no idea he was anywhere near Baton Rouge. Sheer bad luck, one shot in a bloody million."

"Are you sure it was him?"

James nodded. "I've a good head for faces."

"Do you think he saw you?"

"I don't think so. We moved fast."

"What if he did? What would he have done?"

"I'm afraid he and I have an unfortunate history. And he's an unfriendly lad. Plus, he knows Angel Face's da, old man Vitelli. You'd not want to attract his attention."

Teresa leaned against the backrest and let out a slow breath. "But we're safe now?"

"I think so. We'd best put some more miles behind us, though. It's a little under seven hours to San Antonio. Then on to El Paso. We'll either cross there, or keep moving west."

"Tell me about this Mr... Andreotti?"

"You don't want to know."

"Why not?"

He gave her a quick glance. "None of these lads are pleasant. The Fishhook's worse than most."

"Fishhook?"

"You surely know by now, these lads all have nicknames. Angel Face Vitelli, Vinnie the Oil Man, Fishhook Lou Andreotti, and so on."

"Is he a fisherman?" she asked, but she already suspected that wasn't the reason for his title.

"He's a dock worker," James explained. "Or he was, once upon a time. Those lads use longshoreman's hooks to move cargo. You've seen that sort of thing, in pirate films if nowhere else. You know the lads with the eyepatches and the hooks for hands?"

"He's got a hook hand?" she asked, raising her eyebrows. That sounded like something out of a bad horror movie.

"Nothing so dramatic. But he's good with a cargo hook, so they say, and always keeps one about him. Some years back, his crew got in a ruckus with some other Italian lads. Three of theirs disappeared one night. They were found in the hold of one of their own boats the next morning, hanging on hooks through their necks."

Teresa put a hand to her mouth. The barbecue really wasn't sitting easy, and for a second, as she imagined the row of dangling bodies, she thought it was going to come back up. "Why didn't you arrest him?"

"Love, there's a great difference between knowing a lad did something and proving he did it. In this case, there was nothing the coppers could do. Besides, we're talking about things that happened in New Orleans. A New York copper wouldn't have jurisdiction to arrest anyone in Baton Rouge."

"What sort of history do you have?" she asked. "You work in New York, he's a New Orleans crook. How did you even meet?"

"His lot lost a sizable shipment of cargo the last time I was down this way. I fear he holds me responsible."

"Why did we come this way, then?"

"As I said, I'd no idea he'd be in Baton Rouge," James said, a hint of sharpness in his voice. "I can't avoid a whole bloody state simply on the off-chance a lad will walk into the same diner I'm in during the exact same half-hour! It's not like I stay out of New York on account of a few lads I don't want to meet!"

She laid a hand on his arm. "I know. I'm sorry. I'm just frightened."

"You needn't be. He's miles behind us by now, and only getting further away." He smiled at her, and the tension had gone out of his face and voice. "You did well there, love. You're a brave lass."

"Are we all right now?" she asked quietly.

"I'm thinking we are. The rain will make it harder to follow us, even if he saw us, which I'm thinking he didn't."

"Would he? Follow us, I mean?"

James shrugged. "I doubt it. There's no percentage in it."

Teresa tried to relax, but they were two hours west of Baton Rouge before she was able to settle back into her seat.

* * *

"Men are trouble, dear," Norma said. "But they're worth it."

Teresa shook her head. "James isn't like most men," she said. "He's more trouble than most. But this wasn't his fault. At least... I don't think it was. We were doing everything right."

"Every relationship starts with optimism," Norma said. "New love makes you blind to difficulties. I remember what it was like to be young. My husband and I had stars in our eyes for the first three years."

"I know what the world is like," Teresa said, shaking her head. "It may have been optimism, but it wasn't blind. I had... a bad experience, just before I met James. I was scared all the time. Except with him. He had... has this way about him. He makes me want to be brave, and to feel like I can be."

"He sounds like a remarkable man," Norma said. "And a lucky one."

"Him? Lucky? What do you mean?"

"To have found a young woman like you. We should all have someone who sees us the way you see him."

Teresa smiled and blinked her eyes rapidly, clearing the mist she felt collecting. "I'm the lucky one," she said. "Everything was going wrong, and then I met him. And I thought... I thought everything was going to be all right. And it was, for a little while."

Chapter 7

"Teresa?"

"Hmm?" She hadn't meant to fall asleep. She felt like she was swimming through thick, heavy water. She tried to open her eyes. Her eyelids weighed about a ton each.

"We're here, love."

"Huh? Where?"

"San Antonio."

She struggled upright. The rainclouds were gone. The sun was far down in the western sky, shining with the slanting golden light photographers called "magic hour." They were in the parking lot of yet another motel.

"What time is it?" she asked.

"Half past eight. Are you feeling better, love?"

"Yes." She started to get out of the car and winced. Her neck screamed a protest. "No," she corrected herself. "Did you drive straight through?"

"Aye. You must have been tired. You didn't wake when I stopped for petrol about halfway from Baton Rouge. A fright often leaves one tired after it's over. Are you hungry?"

"Maybe in a little while," she said. Her stomach still felt a little funny, maybe from residual adrenaline.

"Then we'll get the room first," he said, opening his door. Teresa gingerly got up and walked stiffly to the lobby behind him. James quickly arranged a room, paying with his apparently inexhaustible roll of cash. Even though it was only on the second floor, they took the elevator in deference to Teresa's discomfort.

"That's the last time I sleep that long in a car," she groaned as James slid the keycard into the lock and let them in.

"Have you ever noticed, these rooms all look the same?" he asked, glancing at the generic décor.

"Maybe it's so you feel at home when you're traveling," she suggested.

"If your home looks like this, love, all I can offer you is my sympathies, and the name of a good interior decorator. I know a lad."

She laughed and winced again. "Oh, God. I've done something to my neck."

"Right," he said, suddenly businesslike. "On the bed, now. Take off your shirt."

"What?" She whirled indignantly and wished she hadn't.

He grinned then. "Teresa, you've seen how I go about charming a lass, and I don't do it like this. My intentions are clean as the Virgin's conscience. If you're wanting to keep your shirt on, be my guest. But my hands work better on bare skin. If you'd care to lie down on your belly, I'll see if I can work some of the kinks out of your neck."

"Oh." What he was saying made sense, but still... "Turn around," she ordered.

Still grinning, James obediently faced the wall. Teresa turned her own back on him while she unbuttoned her blouse. She hung it over the back of a chair and considered her bra.

Then she decided, in for a penny, in for a pound, and unbuckled it. She felt her cheeks flush as she did, marveling at her own boldness. Bare from the waist up, she lay gingerly down on her stomach on top of the comforter.

"Okay," she said.

She was too stiff to turn her head more than a little, so she couldn't see his face. She felt the mattress shift with his weight. His knee brushed against her thigh on one side. Then his other knee came down on the other side of her. He was straddling her, sitting just below her hips. She felt incredibly vulnerable, with this man she still scarcely knew on top of her, looking down at her bare back. She started to shift her weight, instinctively wanting to get free.

He laid his hands on her back, just under her shoulder-blades. The shock of warm skin on skin made her freeze in place. She was struck once again by the incredible warmth radiating from him. His hands slid up her back on either side of her spine. His strong, clever fingers explored the place where her neck met her shoulder, probing gently. She winced and gasped as he found the knot. He began to massage it, starting very lightly and gradually moving deeper and harder, working the tight muscles loose.

"How's that, love?" he asked after a few minutes.

"Mmm," Teresa murmured into the comforter. His touch was lovely. "You've done this before."

"Aye, once or twice." He shifted his grip to her shoulders. "But everyone's different. You have to learn the body you're touching. That's part of the fun, come to that." He kneaded the muscles at the tops of her shoulders.

Teresa sighed. A marvelous feeling of relaxation and wellbeing radiated everywhere he touched her. She hadn't even known how much tension she'd been carrying. James gave her a lengthy massage, giving every part of her back his attention. He was patient and skillful, his hands gentle but strong.

"Aren't you getting tired?" she asked after what seemed a very long time.

"Love, if you think I'd weary of touching you, I fear you're mistaken," he said. "But if you're wanting me to stop..."

"No," she said lazily. "But it seems unfair. You're the one who drove all day, and now you're giving me all this attention. I feel selfish."

"Now that you mention it," he said, "I'd not object to some reciprocity. It's kind of you to offer."

"Okay," she said, somewhat reluctantly. "You'd better get off of me, then, and it'll be your turn to...ooh!"

What she'd been about to say turned into a soft cry of surprise. James had leaned forward, slipped his hands around her body, and cupped her bare breasts. He pressed his chest against her back and held her there, his fingers making small, delicious movements.

Teresa arched against him. She couldn't help it. Her breath escaped her in a shuddering exhalation. What she'd felt the previous night, and tried to push out of her mind, rushed back with a force that astonished her with its suddenness and strength. She moaned softly as he caressed her.

"Oh God, James," she said. "Don't..." She had no idea whether she was telling him to stop, or not to stop.

"Apologies, love," he said. He drew back and swung his leg off of her.

She felt that same sense of mingled disappointment and relief, and wondered how her body could be so at odds with itself. She carefully raised her head, most of the stiffness gone from her neck. James had turned his back again and was unbuttoning his shirt. He tossed it on top of hers on the chair with a quick, casual movement. She reflected that he had expensive tastes for a police officer. The shirt was definitely silk, costing more than most things in her wardrobe at home. He peeled off his undershirt and sent it after the other garment. Then he lay down on his own stomach beside her.

"Ready when you are, love," he said. His head was turned away in an uncharacteristic gesture of modesty.

Teresa pushed herself up to her knees and looked down at James's body. It was the first chance she'd had to study him when he wasn't returning the favor. She put out a hand and saw the contrast between her olive complexion and his pale skin. A spray of freckles speckled his upper back. On his left shoulder, wrapped around the upper arm, was a complicated Celtic tattoo of intertwining lines. Just above his right hip, on his lower back, he had a perfectly circular scar, three inches across. There were two more scars she could see, a puckered one about a half-inch in diameter on his right triceps, and a fine line across his ribs.

She traced the circle on his back with a fingertip.

"Careful, love," he said. "That tickles a bit."

"What is this?" she asked, indulging her schoolteacher's instinct to learn.

"Oh, you needn't trouble about that. I was in a wee set-to in a pub, some years back. A lad found my back turned and took the opportunity to stick me with a broken bottle."

Teresa flinched sympathetically. "Oh, dear," she said. Then she touched the line on his ribs. "What about this one?"

"That's a ruffian with a knife," he said. "I'm quicker than most, but that lad was fast and lucky. I'm fortunate he only slashed me a bit. This is important, Terry. If you're ever in a knife-fight, use the point, not the edge. Cutting a lad won't stop him. It'll only make him angry. You want to stop him, you need to stab, nice and deep. Like you mean it."

"What happened to him? The man who cut you?"

"I took his knife away from him," James said. "And I taught him a few things about using it. But that's an unpleasant story, and I'm thinking you're not wanting the details."

Teresa swallowed. "And this?" she asked, putting a fingertip on the mark on his right arm.

"Oh, that wee thing? It's from a bullet."

"James, you were shot?" she exclaimed, horrified.

"Aye, just the once. There's a matching one on the other side of the arm. Went in and out, missed the bone. Best place to be shot, really. Nothing important to be damaged."

"Except your arm!"

"Aye, but I've two of those."

Teresa shook her head. "You're impossible. Didn't it hurt?"

"If it's not happening now, pain's in the past, love."

"Isn't pleasure the same way?" she couldn't resist replying.

He did turn his head then to look at her then. "Aye," he said, his eyes twinkling. "But I'd hardly call this situation painful." His eyes slid away from her face.

Then Teresa remembered she wasn't wearing anything above the waist. Her mouth dropped open and she reflexively put an arm across her chest. "James!" she exclaimed.

"You needn't worry, love," he said. "I've liked everything I've seen of you. No need to be hiding."

Quickly, to cover her growing embarrassment, she straddled his hips, sitting on him and forcing his slender frame down. In this position he'd have trouble looking at her. He lay quietly under her. She began massaging his back as he'd done to her. She was a little discombobulated, so her attentions were less self-assured than his, but he didn't seem to mind.

She found the knots in his shoulders, the tension he hid under his carefree façade, and worked her thumbs into them. He sucked in air through his teeth.

"I'm not hurting you, am I?" she asked.

"Nay, I'm fine," he said. "Sometimes you need to feel worse to feel better. A little torture focuses the mind."

His words ended on an exclamation as she dug her right thumb in a little harder. "You were saying?" she asked sweetly.

He chuckled quietly. "You'd be a half-decent interrogator, love. Here's me, at your mercy."

"Then start talking," she said. "What are your intentions?"

"I'm to get you safe to Mexico."

"That wasn't quite what I meant." She stopped kneading his muscles, laid her hands flat against his back, and slid her palms over him. She felt the muscle in his slim body and felt a little shiver in her lower belly. He really was the most attractive man she'd ever been near.

"You need to be more particular with your questions," he said. "If you're ever hoping for a second career with the coppers, that is."

"Okay." She caressed his shoulders and upper arms, marveling at the feel of his skin. "Do you think I'm pretty?"

"Teresa," he said, "any red-blooded lad who likes the lasses would think you're pretty. And my blood's as red as the next man's."

"Do you want to..." she paused, looking for the right words, and felt herself blushing again. She wished she wasn't so easily embarrassed. Here she was, half-naked, sitting on top of a man, and she was worrying about saying the wrong thing.

"Do I want what?" he asked.

"Do you want to be with me?"

"Don't you think that's obvious, love? I know you've not much experience with the lads, but as I'm sure you're aware, there's certain indicators."

Teresa felt herself go red right to the ears, blood rushing into her face. "Then why haven't you?" she asked.

James went very still underneath her. "I beg your pardon?" he said, and she knew he was stalling for time.

"You want to sleep with me," she said, feeling bolder as she sensed his sudden awkwardness. "You could've had me yesterday. Maybe earlier. You're confident with women. You know what you want and how to get it. You've been trying to win me over ever since I got into your car. And it's not like I can get away from you. I'm depending on you. No one in the world knows where we are right now. You could do anything you want with me."

The truth of that statement sank into her as she said it, an intoxicating mix of fear and exhilaration shooting straight through the middle of her. Her desire for him was so strong that she felt dizzy. If she'd been standing, her legs might have buckled.

James twisted under her. The swiftness of the motion caught her off guard, and before she knew what he was doing, he'd flipped onto his back and was facing her. Her legs still straddled him just above the hips. She could feel every bit of him, even through both layers of their pants.

"And is that what you're wanting?" he asked softly. She felt his eyes on her naked skin, almost as if they were touching her. Unconsciously, she shifted restlessly. She wanted him to touch her. It was like a thirst in her flesh.

"I don't know," she whispered.

"Are you frightened?" he asked.

"No." Then, after the briefest hesitation, "Yes."

"So am I," he said, and looked surprised to hear himself admit it.

"You?" she exclaimed, startled.

"Well, not precisely," he said, a self-conscious grin spreading across his face. "But I'm experiencing something a bit outside my personal frame of reference, if you know what I mean."

She shook her head. "Everything that's happened to me this week has been outside my frame of reference."

He laughed. "Aye, that's a good point. What I mean is, I was thinking to seduce you, the moment I laid eyes on you."

"James!"

"Well, as you've said, it would've been convenient. A few days, even weeks, just the two of us, on the road together? A romantic adventure, something for us both to look back on and smile. I'd no intention of taking you against your will, love. I've never had a lass who wasn't full willing, and I'd never do such a thing. But I'll admit I've been trying my best to win you over."

Without fully realizing she was doing it, Teresa laid her hands on James's stomach. There were more scars on his chest, and surely a story to go with every one, but they didn't make him less attractive. They made the map of his skin more interesting, the way cities in an atlas had layers of history underneath them.

"You've been doing a good job," she said.

He nodded. His own hands came up and caressed her sides. She shivered and bit her lower lip. "I'd a plan at the start," he said. "But that's gone out the window. Oh, I'll get you to Mexico, and I'll keep you safe, but as far as you and me, love... that's in the wind."

Teresa's hand slid up to his chest. She felt his intake of breath through his whole frame and settled herself more fully against him. They were teasing each other, she realized, both of them helpless to stop, coming closer and closer to the edge of control. It was dangerous, maybe, but that was part of the thrill, too. "You want me so badly," she said, and wondered at the husky tone in her own voice. "What's the problem?"

"You're trusting me," he said quietly. "I don't want to let you down. The way you've looked at me, from the start... you believe in me, and you make me want to believe it too."

"Believe what?" she whispered.

His hands stopped moving, resting on her waist. "That I'm not a bad man," he said in a voice so low she had to bend forward to hear it.

Teresa stared at him, still leaning close so their faces were only a few inches apart. "You're a good man, James," she said. "I can't be the only person who sees it."

James Corcoran actually looked frightened. In that moment, he looked much younger than he was, almost like a scared teenager. He shook his head.

"Everyone's always thought the worst of me," he said. "Even back when I was a wee bairn. And when people expect the worst, you'd be surprised how often they bring it out. Don't fall in love with me, Teresa."

That last sentence stopped her cold. "Why not?"

"I'll hurt you. I'll break your heart."

She took hold of one of his hands and pressed it to her chest, between her breasts. "No you won't," she said. "You promised you'd protect me. You won't hurt me. I do trust you."

"For all you've seen of the world, lass, you're almost too innocent to be breathing," he said. "The people we trust are always the ones who hurt us the most."

"But you won't."

He considered her, but she realized he was looking inward at the same time, examining his own soul. "Nay," he said quietly, talking as much to himself as to her. "I won't. Not if I can help it."

His hand was still pressed against her chest, just over her heart. It moved outward, gently, caressing her breast. She shivered again.

"Anything you're not wanting," he said quietly, "I'll not do. Just tell me and I'll stop. You understand?"

She nodded. The air in the room was suddenly very hard to breathe. Her heart beat faster. Her blood felt hot, as if her whole body was simmering. She thought, incongruously, of her mother's kitchen, of tomato sauce bubbling in the pot, and giggled.

The laughter was cut off as James sat up swiftly, curling his upper body against hers with a strength she hadn't suspected in his slender frame. She could feel every inch of him, skin to skin. Then he was kissing her and nothing else seemed important anymore. His lips were soft but demanding, caressing her mouth. She felt the tip of his tongue, teasing her. She opened her mouth and let him in.

Some tiny part of her was still afraid, but she could no longer tell the difference between fear and excitement, and it only served to heighten her sensations. His lips traveled from her mouth to her neck, her shoulders, her chest. His hands were everywhere at once, and every touch only made her want more.

He laid her down on her back and unbuttoned her jeans. She raised her hips and let him slide them down her legs. He moved his hands up her thighs. Then he was doing things she'd never even imagined. She didn't know what to expect, and the fear and excitement built up in her unbearably. It went on and on, lifting her higher with every moment.

Then she felt herself explode into a thousand tiny fragments. She'd known what unbearable pain felt like; she'd never imagined unbearable pleasure. She felt wetness on her cheeks and knew she was weeping, didn't know why, and didn't care.

"Are you all right, love?" James asked.

She had no idea how to answer him. Dumbly, she nodded. He was poised above her, a look of strained expectancy on his face.

"Are you ready?" he asked.

What sort of question was that? Ready for what? What could possibly come that hadn't already happened? But she nodded again.

There was a little pain, a short, sharp jolt of jarring sensation, but he paused at that moment, holding himself still, letting her get used to the strangeness of the impossible closeness of their contact. She opened her eyes, without realizing she'd closed them, and all she saw in his face was a soft tenderness that brought fresh tears to her eyes. She put up a trembling hand and touched his cheek.

Slowly, gently, he began to move against her, inside her. Teresa's body knew what to do better than she did, teaching her a dance older than humanity itself. She rose against him, fitting herself into every curve and hollow of his scarred, beautiful body, and lost herself in the rhythm. There was another explosion, and another, and she thought maybe death might feel like that, but if it did, she wasn't afraid of it anymore.

*   *   *

Afterward, he held her. She could feel a hesitation in him, something not quite right. But he was gentle and loving, and resting in his arms she was as comfortable as she could ever remember being.

"How are you feeling, Terry?" he asked,

"No one calls me Terry," she murmured. She wriggled into a closer position, nestling against him.

"Ah, grand. Then it's something special for us to share. Are you hurting at all? Sometimes, the first time, it's a bit difficult."

She was a little sore, to be honest, but it didn't bother her. It was like the ache that came after healthy exercise, muscles letting her know they'd done what she'd asked, but it was time to rest now. "Sleepy," she said. She'd gone from fear to exhilaration to exhaustion.

"Sleep, then," he whispered. "I'll hold you."

"All night?"

"If that's what you're wanting. I'll stay beside you and keep off the bad dreams. I'll be here when you wake, you've my word."

As she drifted off, the last thought she remembered was that she wasn't going to be able to follow his advice. It was already too late. She'd fallen in love with him.

*   *   *

"What are you smiling about, dear?" Norma asked.

"Remembering," Teresa said.

"When I was a girl," Norma said, "we'd say that was the smile of a cat that had got the canary."

"Maybe," she said. "But I don't know which of us was the cat, and which was the bird."

"The games we play," Norma said. "I notice you aren't wearing a ring."

"What?" Teresa was caught completely off guard.

Norma nodded toward her hand, which felt suddenly naked and empty. "He hasn't popped the question yet?"

Teresa wished, for probably the thousandth time, that she didn't blush so easily. "James... does not commit to things easily. Or to people."

"Is he a keeper?"

"Maybe. If he'll let himself be kept."

Chapter 8

She woke to a feather-light touch, so gentle it felt like the trailing edge of a dream. Delicious, tingling warmth radiated through her whole body. Something large, warm, and comfortable lay against her back. She nestled against it with a sigh.

The light touch grew stronger, more urgent. Teresa's head cleared a little. She'd had the most amazing dream. She'd dreamed that she and James had... oh, it had been bad, but so, so good.

"Terry? Are you awake, love?"

The words were whispered against the back of her neck, so close that she felt James's lips on her skin. With that, she came fully alert, remembering it hadn't been a dream. James was in bed with her, his whole length pressed to her, and she realized, with a not altogether unpleasant shock, neither of them was wearing anything.

He felt her stiffen and became immediately concerned. "Terry? You're all right, aren't you?"

"I... um... yes," she said. It seemed a very inadequate description of her state of mind and body, but she didn't have anything better to add. "James? What are you doing here?"

"I promised," he said, sounding a little confused. "I said I'd be here when you woke, and I'm a lad of my word."

"That's not..." she began, then forgot what she was saying. His hand was moving again, down below her waist, and she felt a sudden surge of desire so strong it drowned out everything else. She gasped and moved involuntarily against him. Then he was doing things to her, some of them the same as the night before, some new, all of them exhilarating.

"My goodness," she said at last, when they had finished. Her voice was shaky.

He laughed. "I'll take that as a compliment, love."

"My mother warned me, when I was a teenager, that boys only wanted one thing from a girl," she said.

He cocked an eyebrow. "Now that's simply not true," he said in self-righteous tones.

"Really?" She answered with an eyebrow of her own. "What else do you want, then?"

"There's home cooking," he said with a wink.

"James! This is the twenty-first century! Women aren't just in the kitchen and the... the bedroom!" She knew he was teasing her, but she couldn't quite stop her indignation.

He grinned. "Oh, we needn't confine ourselves. We can do this in the living room, in the bath, on the dining table, anywhere you choose."

"James!"

"I like the way you say my name," he said.

"You do?" She was surprised.

"Aye."

"But I'm usually scolding you."

"That's true," he admitted. "But you say it like you're expecting better of me. It makes me want to be better."

"But you don't improve. You just keep on being you."

"Isn't that enough for you, love?"

"We should always try to be better for the people we care about."

"I was good for you a few moments ago," he said and slipped his hand between her thighs.

"Don't you ever have enough?" she demanded, but she didn't pull away or slap his hand aside.

"If I do, I'll be sure to tell you," he murmured, bending in to kiss her.

"Don't we have things to do?"

"Oh aye, quite a number of them. Would you like me to describe them, or simply pitch right in?"

"I'm talking about escaping to Mexico. Or maybe having breakfast, at least?"

He laughed. "Aye, whatever you're wanting, love. But we're in no rush. After all, no one even knows we're in El Paso."

"There was that guy in Baton Rouge," she reminded him. "What's his name? Lou something?"

"Aye, but we only nibbled the Fishhook's bait and swam away," James said. "He's no notion where we've gone, if he even noticed us in the first place."

"You're right," she said distractedly. James was doing a little nibbling of his own at that moment, on her earlobe and the side of her neck. "You're in charge of this trip," she said. Her voice was breathier than usual and it was hard to get out the words. "It's... your... decision."

"Let's give it another half hour," he said. "Then a shower and breakfast. We'll be needing both, I'm thinking. The road will wait. You'd be surprised what you can do with a half hour."

She was.

*   *   *

On the road again, northbound toward Las Cruces on Highway 10, Teresa felt like she was flying. The scenery was uninteresting: dry grass and mesquite, chain-link fencing, and small, single-story houses, all unfamiliar to her city-bred eyes. But the wide-open spaces and brilliant blue sky seemed to hold nothing but the promise of good things.

She kept replaying the events of the last twenty-four hours in her mind. She wanted to burn every moment, every feeling into her memory. Even now, some of it felt more like a dream than reality. She looked at James, tracing every line of his face with her eyes. He glanced back at her and smiled.

"Terry, love, you're going to have to pace yourself."

"What do you mean?"

"The way you're looking at me, if you do half the things you're thinking, there'll be nothing left of me by the time we get to Mexico."

She felt the now-familiar rush of blood to her cheeks. "James! I wasn't going to... I mean, I was just... remembering."

He grinned. "That's grand, love. A lad told me once, memory's the best cinema you can have. It's free, it's always open, and if you don't like what's playing, you can change the story to fit your feelings."

"Maybe that's how your memory works," she said. "With mine, I don't always like what's on the screen."

"Are you referring to the late unpleasantness with Angel Face?"

"And the car bomb."

He nodded. "Those are part of you now, true enough. But you've got to put them behind you. I find it's best not to try to forget. That never works, not even with alcoholic assistance. It's better to simply add new memories, good ones. Fill yourself up with those, and they can crowd out the ugliness."

"Is that what we're doing?" she said, putting a hand on his leg. "Making good memories?"

The car drifted across the center line. "Steady, love," he said. "You mustn't distract the driver."

"What's the most distracted you've ever been while driving?" she asked, leaving her hand where it was.

"Terry, that's no story for mixed company."

"James! You haven't had... you know... you haven't been with a girl while driving. Have you?"

"Never..." he began.

"Good," she said prematurely.

"...within city limits," he finished.

"What difference does that make?"

"Cruise control," he explained. "It's much safer on the interstate."

"James!"

"Want me to demonstrate?" He engaged the cruise control and kept his left hand on the steering wheel.

"James! What are you doing?" Teresa cried. His other hand was wandering. "James! Watch the road!" She slapped his hand.

He laughed and returned his hands to the wheel. "No harm done, love. I was just making a point. It's perfectly possible."

"Distracted driving causes as many accidents as alcohol," she said. "Probably more."

"So you're saying I should drink instead?"

"No!" But she couldn't help smiling with him. "You're incorrigible. You're like a little boy."

"Whenever possible. Boys have more fun than men." The smile stayed on his mouth but faded a little from his eyes. "But I can be a man, when I have to be." Then the sparkle was back, like the sun coming out from behind a cloud. "I just hope it's not too common a necessity."

"James, I have a question."

"Fire away, love."

"We're going to Mexico, right?"

"Aye."

"But we're going north now. Why?"

"Only about thirty miles. Highway 10 turns west in Las Cruces. Then we'll hit Tucson, keep on south of Phoenix, through Yuma to San Diego. That's where we'll cross."

"But we could have crossed the border back in El Paso. Why didn't we?"

"Two reasons, love."

She waited for him to elaborate.

"First, the roads this side of the border are brilliant compared with the ones south of here. We can count on regular petrol stations, good blacktop, and reasonably courteous fellow drivers."

"That's four reasons."

"Nay, that's all part of the first," he said. "The second is, if we crossed at El Paso, we'd be in Ciudad Juarez."

"So?"

"You remember, back in New York, the worst neighborhoods? Hunts Point? Tremont?"

"Bedford-Stuyvesant," she added.

"Aye. Think of them: the tenements, the drug dealers, the dirt, the crime. Now imagine, if you can, a whole city like that, only more so."

"I see," she said.

"Nay, it's worse than that," he continued. "Now imagine the drug cartels are running the whole place. A woman or girl is murdered every day, on average. That's not even counting the lads who buy it, some of them in the trade, some innocent.

There's thousands of coppers in the city, but they're only adding to the trouble. The Mexican government put one of their generals into the place a few years back, to set things in order, but then he got himself arrested on murder charges."

"Oh," Teresa said quietly.

"So we'll not be going through Juarez," he finished. "There's much nicer parts of Mexico I'd prefer to show you."

"Have you ever been there?"

"Mexico? Aye, more than once."

"No, Ciudad Juarez."

"Aye, a few years back." James shook his head. "Things are actually a bit better now. Back then, it had the highest murder rate. I don't mean simply in North America, Terry. It was the highest in the whole bloody world."

"What were you doing there?"

"Working."

She could see he didn't want to talk about it. "San Diego sounds nice," she said, changing the subject.

"It's grand. And so is Baja. It's much lovelier than central Mexico. I'm looking forward to your face when you stand on a beach for the first time, looking at the Pacific Ocean. I'm going to bring you to the shore at sunset, when the sky's painted all manner of orange, red, and purple. I'll gather you in my arms, there on the sand, and kiss you, and then take you into your house, lay you down on your bed, and make love to you with the sea breeze stirring the curtains."

She blinked. "You've put some thought into this."

"Oh, aye," he said. "It's grand having things to look forward to."

"You don't seem like much of a long-term planner, usually."

"Looking forward to something's not the same as planning it. I like to be surprised as much as the next lad."

"How comforting."

"Look, Terry, I've planned out the important things," he said. "The house is waiting, we've all our papers in order, false identities, money, all of it. The surprises are in the little things."

"How have you been surprised so far this trip?" she asked.

"You've surprised me."

"Is that so?"

"I didn't expect to like you quite so much."

"But you were planning on sleeping with me."

He grinned. "Can you really blame me for that?"

"What if you hadn't liked me?"

"That's not possible."

"I mean, what if I were different?" she pressed. "Or if you were? Once you'd seduced me, what would you have done then?"

He wasn't smiling anymore. "I'd have taken care of you regardless," he said. "I admit, I'm a lad who mixes business with pleasure when he can, but I do know the difference. My business is to see no harm comes to you."

"Even if there are more surprises?"

"No matter what."

*   *   *

The airplane lurched suddenly, sickeningly. Someone in the cabin gave a short exclamation of surprise. With a pinging sound, the seat belt lights came on.

"Attention," a voice came over the speakers. "This is the captain speaking. We are experiencing some turbulence. Please remain seated, with your seat belts fastened."

"It doesn't matter how much planning you do," Teresa said to Norma. "Something can always throw things off."

"That's true enough," Norma said. "I used to think I had my whole life laid out. Now, looking back, it doesn't look anything like I'd intended."

"Is it better?" Teresa asked. "Or worse?"

"A bit of both, dear. But I wouldn't change a single day. Without all of them, I wouldn't be where I am today."

"And where is that?"

"Talking to a nice young woman while I'm traveling to visit my family. What could be better than that?"

Teresa nodded, but she knew the worry was showing on her face again. "I would change some things," she said quietly.

Norma put out a hand and laid it on her arm. "What happened, dear?"

"James saw a man he knew on the road," she said. "In a restaurant. It seems like a very long time ago now. I can't really explain it. I suppose the details aren't important anyway. We thought it didn't matter. But it did. It changed everything."

Chapter 9

Las Cruces was a bigger city than Teresa expected, but that wasn't saying much. She'd always pictured New Mexico as being basically empty. Finding anything but desert came as something of a surprise.

James, of course, had an anecdote about the place. Like most of his stories, it had to do with transportation. "Have you heard of Spaceport America, love?" he asked.

She shook her head. "What is it, some kind of theme park?"

He laughed. "You could call it that. It's the tallest, most expensive amusement-park ride in the world. It's the first place designed and built from the ground up as a private spaceport."

"As in, rocket ships?"

"More along the lines of very high-flying airplanes. They opened only a couple of years ago. I've been meaning to take a trip up."

"How much does that cost?" she asked.

"Fifty to a hundred, give or take."

"Fifty dollars isn't so bad. You should do that."

"Thousand, love."

"*Fifty thousand dollars?*"

"I've been thinking the price may come down, so I've been biding my time. I don't want to be excessive."

"That's only a little less than I make in a year," she said, dazed. "Before taxes."

"Ah, but that's for a flight of six," he said. "Split six ways, we're under ten grand apiece. That's a bit more within reach. Would you like to come up with me?"

"Into space?"

"Why not?"

"James, I absolutely forbid you to spend ten thousand dollars to fly me into space."

"Experience of a lifetime, love."

"If you want to spend ten thousand dollars on a vacation, take me somewhere warm," she said.

"Like Mexico?"

She smiled. "That will do just fine. I'm not a fancy girl, James. I thought you liked that about me."

"I do. But surely I'm permitted to make an extravagant gesture or two."

They stopped for a bite to eat at a pizza place just off the interstate, a simple family restaurant. Then they were back on the road, heading west into the desert of the American Southwest. Four hours took them clear across New Mexico and into Tucson, Arizona. By the time they rolled into the city limits, Teresa was finally and completely overwhelmed by the sheer size of America.

"I used to think New York was big," she said.

"So it is, love," James said. "Biggest city in America."

"But there's just so much... everything out here," she said, waving a hand at the windshield.

"Things are more spread out in these parts," he said. "Think of Ireland, Terry. The entire island's got a population about the same as New York City. In the city, you can have more adventures going four blocks than you can going four hundred miles out here."

Teresa nodded. "You're right. It does stretch out. Everything west of the Mississippi seems that way."

"Are you tired, love?"

"A little stiff."

"Sounds like someone's angling for another massage."

She giggled. "I wouldn't complain."

"Nor I. We'll find a place to stay, and I promise to make you extremely comfortable."

Teresa didn't say anything. She thought back to the previous night. She was discovering the combination of memory and anticipation could be a very powerful mixture. She shivered with an unexpected rush of desire for the talkative, mysterious, scarred, beautiful man sitting next to her.

*   *   *

James took them off the Interstate toward the Tucson Airport, proclaiming the airport hotels to be better than the roadside motels. It added a little more driving time, but given the amount of time they'd already spent on the road the past few days, Teresa hardly noticed. It was still a little early for dinner, with plenty of daylight.

"Should we push on?" she asked. "We could do a few more miles."

He shrugged. "We're in no hurry. Besides, you've got me thinking about the feel of your skin under my hands again, and I'm finding my interest in driving sadly diminished by comparison."

She laughed. "You have a one-track mind."

"I've noticed most lads do, when it comes to this manner of thing. But I'm making other plans, too. What do you say to me bringing you dinner in our room, as we did night before last?"

"That sounds… grand," she said, mimicking his accent. "I can get cleaned up while you get the food."

"Grand," he echoed.

They got a room at the Doubletree Suites on the second floor and moved their luggage in. The room was a little old compared with their previous accommodations, but comfortable. James took one of the keys and tucked it in his pocket. "I'll be back in a half hour," he said, giving her a lingering kiss that promised much more to come. "What is it you're wanting to eat?"

"Surprise me," she said.

He grinned. "With pleasure."

Once he was gone, Teresa went into the bathroom. The tub was on the small side, so she had a nice, long shower instead. She washed her hair and then just stood in the hot water, letting it run down her neck and shoulders.

Was she really in love with James? She didn't know for sure; how could she? Everything about her situation was new and unfamiliar. She couldn't deny how he made her feel, and it wasn't just the way her body responded to him. Though she had to admit that was definitely a large part of it. He was funny, kind, and friendly. She couldn't imagine traveling so far in the company of anyone else without going a little crazy. Even her family would have had her clawing her way out of the car by now.

She knew it was a bad idea. He'd even told her it was. He was a professional, doing his job, protecting her. She shouldn't compromise that. It could get both of them in trouble. In fact, he'd probably already compromised himself. If she reported him to Detective O'Reilly, he'd certainly face disciplinary action. A police officer wasn't supposed to sleep with the woman he was guarding. Of course, the forbidden nature of their relationship only added another layer of desire.

Oh, but she wanted him to come back, to put her arms around him, to feel that achingly pleasurable rhythm of their bodies. She'd never known she could want someone so badly. All these years of living single, never dating seriously, and she'd never understood what all the fuss was about. Now she wanted to pounce on James the moment he came through the door.

Teresa turned off the water and wrapped one towel around her body, another around her hair like a turban. She briefly considered what to wear. Then she smiled at herself in the mirror.

"This will do just fine," she said, enjoying the mischievous gleam she saw in her own eyes. It reminded her of the sparkle in James's. She went out to the main room and lay down on the bed, still clad only in the towels, to wait for her man.

She'd only been lying there a few minutes when she heard the lock click on the door. She rose up on one elbow in what she hoped was a flattering, inviting pose, and put on her best coy smile.

"Miss me?" she asked as the door opened.

The bottom dropped out of her stomach. The man in the doorway was not James Corcoran.

*   *   *

Time froze. Teresa saw a well-built guy, big in the shoulders, wearing a tight black T-shirt that showed off impressively muscled arms. He was olive-skinned and black-haired, crew-cut and clean-shaven. He was obviously, undeniably Italian.

He stared back at her. His eyes reminded her of something from childhood. Her parents had taken her to the New York Aquarium when she'd been ten. She remembered the sandbar sharks, particularly their dull eyes, like black marbles. Expressionless, inhuman, terrifying.

The man stepped into the room then, sweeping the door shut behind him with his left hand. He kept watching her, without blinking.

"I think you have the wrong room," Teresa said, and to her surprise, the words came out almost natural—just a little higher pitched than usual.

He shook his head and changed expression for the first time. He smiled. It was a normal-looking smile, even a friendly one, except for his eyes. They didn't change at all, and they made the smile unnatural, grotesque. "I don't think so," he said. His voice was soft, almost warm.

Teresa was very aware she was wearing only a towel around her, and another on her hair. She felt naked under those awful eyes. She sat up and scooted back on the bed, trying to put more space between them. Her glance darted to James's duffel bag. He'd have taken his knife with him, but maybe he had another weapon in there, maybe even a gun. She knew almost immediately that it didn't matter. There was no time. She couldn't expect this man to just stand there while she rummaged for a gun that might or might not be there. Besides, she didn't even know how to use one, and it might not be loaded.

The man kept coming at a slow, easy pace, as if he had all the time in the world.

"What do you want?" she asked. She meant it to be a quick, sharp question, like her mom used with door-to-door salesmen, but this time her voice betrayed her. The fear shone through. He was going to kill her, of course. The Mafia had found her, somehow, and now she was going to die, for real this time, alone in this airport hotel room.

He paused. A look of polite confusion crossed his face. "Me? Oh, I was just hoping we could talk for a bit, while we wait for your boy to come back."

"Talk?" she repeated weakly. She felt a sudden, dizzying surge of hope that maybe, just maybe she was mistaken. Maybe this was all some misunderstanding. There were plenty of Italian-Americans who weren't in the Mob. She was one of them herself.

"Yeah," he said. He stepped around the foot of the bed. Teresa shrank against the headboard, curling her legs under herself. "Hey, don't worry. I'm not gonna hurt you. Who'd want to hurt a nice girl like you? You're Italian, right? You from the old country, or born here?"

"I... I was born here," she said. "My grandparents came over."

He nodded. Then, to her astonishment, he sat down on the edge of the bed beside her, just as if they were old friends. "No kidding!" he said. "Mine, too. Your people from Italy, or Sicily?"

"Italy," she said. "Around Naples."

He nodded. "Mine are from Sicily. Palermo. You got a New York accent, bambolina. Is that where Corky picked you up?"

She froze. He knew James. She thought of the restaurant in Baton Rouge, of the man he'd seen there. But they'd shaken him, James had been sure of it. How could he have followed them all this way?

"Fishhook Lou," she blurted out without thinking.

He blinked. Then his smile came back, wider than before. Now she could see the tips of his teeth between his lips, and it didn't even look friendly on the surface. He looked more like a shark than ever.

"We met, babe? I think I'd remember a face like this." He put out his left hand and lightly caressed her cheek.

She trembled at his touch. She knew she should hit him, run away, do *something*, but his eyes held her. She thought of animals again. He wasn't a shark after all. He was a snake, hypnotizing her like they did to birds. Teresa was frightened in a way she'd never been frightened before, not when the car bomb went off, not even when she'd seen Angel Face Vitelli outside her apartment.

He kept stroking her cheek. "Easy, babe. Don't worry, this'll all be over soon."

Teresa whimpered. She couldn't help herself.

"Me and Corky just have some business to take care of," he said. "It's okay, I know he's out. I watched him leave. I can wait. When's he coming back?"

She couldn't speak. It wasn't that she was determined not to give him information. Courage had nothing to do with it. Her brain and her lips just couldn't form words. She shook her head mutely, staring wide-eyed at him.

Still smiling, still stroking her cheek, Lou reached behind his back with his right hand. He brought it out again, and when she saw what he was holding, her heart lurched in her chest.

It was a long, curved steel cargo hook.

"Babe, don't make this any worse than it needs to be," he said, his voice still soft and almost kind. "I got no beef with you. But when Corky comes back, things are gonna get a little unpleasant, so I need you to help me out here. We can do it easy, or hard. We do it hard, he's not gonna like what he sees when he comes in here."

Without warning, he curled the fingers of his left hand up under the towel on her head and twined them into her hair. He pulled sharply, jerking her head to one side. Teresa gave a short gasp of shock and pain. Then she felt the cold metal tip of the hook under her chin. She tried not to move, fighting the urge to reflexively swallow.

Lou brought his face right up to hers, so he was staring into her terrified eyes from a distance of less than three inches. "I'm not gonna have a problem with you, am I, *puta*?" he asked, calling her a whore in the same pleasant, soft voice he'd been using when he'd asked about her family.

Teresa shook her head as much as she dared, trying to pull away from the hook.

"Good, good," he said. "Now, when's Corky coming back?"

"Soon," she whispered, trying to talk without moving her jaw. "He said... half an hour."

Lou nodded. "Good. Now here's what we're gonna do. We're going back in the bathroom. Get up now."

He kept holding her head with his left hand, gripping her hair near the roots. The hook traveled around her throat, stopping just under her right ear. Lou pulled her to her feet. For a second Teresa thought her legs might buckle, but knew if she fainted, Lou would probably kill her, would just drive the hook through the artery in her neck and rip the life out of her. She had to be strong, had to stay alive.

They went to the bathroom. Lou pushed her in ahead of him and nudged the door shut with his hip. "Now run the bathwater," he said. "I know you just took one, but now you're gonna take another."

A new fear hit Teresa. What else might Lou do to her? What if he had rape on his mind? But no, he wouldn't risk that, not with James coming back any minute. But then why tell her to do this? She didn't dare ask. Obediently, she turned on the hot water and started filling the tub.

Lou let go of her and stood back against the door. He crossed his arms and watched her. "Who are you, anyway?" he asked. "What's your name, babe?"

Teresa blinked. If he didn't know who she was, then why was he here? Her mind raced. She wasn't a good liar. "Linda," she said, snatching at the name of one of her childhood friends, a girl she'd lost touch with years ago. "Linda Moretti."

"Pleased to meet you, Linda. Now, I don't want you to get the wrong idea, but you're gonna take off that towel and get in that tub."

Teresa wanted to turn away from him, keep him from seeing too much of her, but the thought of taking her eyes off him was somehow worse. She gulped back a sob and unwrapped the towel from her head. Her hair, still wet, fell to her shoulders. It was cold and clammy. She shuddered. She stared at Lou, mutely begging him for mercy.

"Come on, Linda," he said, but without sounding particularly irritated. He went on, in a casual, conversational tone. "Y'know, we can still do this the other way, where I pull your guts out and spread 'em around the room like party streamers. You want it that way?"

Tears of helplessness, fear, and humiliation welled up in her eyes. She fumbled with the other towel and let it fall away from her. She stepped quickly into the tub and sat down in the hot water. She covered herself as well as she could, curling up her legs and clutching her knees.

Lou looked her over dispassionately. "I see why he likes you," he said. "You're a good-looking girl. Hey, hey, don't cry. This'll be over real soon now. Listen to me, Linda. When he comes back, all you gotta do is just one thing. You don't need to say nothing. I don't want you to talk. Just lie there, take one hand and beckon to him. If he's the guy I think he is, that'll be all he needs. Can you do that?"

Teresa stared at him. She wanted to scream that she'd never betray James, not even for her own life, but she was so frightened. She didn't want to die.

Lou sighed. "Look, Linda, either that, or I hook out your eyes and start on the rest of you. We got a deal?"

She shivered again, still curled into a tight ball, and nodded.

He smiled with false warmth. "Good, good. You're a smart girl. Just wait right there."

Lou left the bathroom door open. Across from the bathroom was a closet with a light, folding door. He stepped into the closet and drew the door almost completely shut. As he did, he raised the hook to his mouth and held it to his lips, as if it was a finger, in a shushing motion. Then, grotesquely, he winked at her as if they shared some delightful secret.

Teresa never knew how long she sat there, with the water gradually rising until it was almost at the lip of the tub. She somehow had the presence of mind to turn off the tap before it overflowed. Then, feeling horribly exposed, she waited and tried to think of the best thing to do. She should scream, as soon as James opened the door, a warning. She should tell him to run, to save himself, to get help, to save her.

But then Lou would kill her. She was absolutely sure he would.

Maybe James could protect her. She thought of his careless, easy manner, the incredible speed of his hands, the way he laughed at danger. She remembered the scars on his body. This wouldn't be the first time someone had come after him. Maybe, just maybe, he would be quicker than Lou, tougher. If she warned him at the last minute, who knew what might happen?

And besides, a small, treacherous voice whispered in her brain, maybe Lou wasn't intending to kill anyone. Maybe he just needed to talk to James, to work out some sort of arrangement. Maybe, if she just kept quiet and behaved, everything would somehow work out.

She didn't believe that voice, but it was hard not to reach out for the hope it offered.

In the middle of her thoughts, she heard the metallic click of the room's lock. Jolted out of her worries, she felt a surge of panic. She wasn't ready, not for this. She hadn't made up her mind. But it didn't matter. She was out of time. The door swung open.

James stepped into the bathroom doorway. He was holding a plastic bag in one hand, a bottle tucked under his arm. He shifted the bottle to his other hand and glanced her direction. His smile, so much warmer and more genuine than Lou's, lit up his face.

"Evening, love," he said. "I thought you'd be none the worse for a change, so I've got us some Chinese. I thought surely you'd be done with your bath by now. You must be half mermaid."

Teresa tried to open her mouth, to find her courage and warn him, but her tongue refused to obey her. Hating herself for a coward, she raised a hand and crooked a finger at him, just like Lou had told her to.

The briefest shadow of confusion or uncertainty crossed over his face as he looked into her eyes. "Everything all right, love? If you're not wanting Chinese, I can fetch something else. I thought everyone liked egg rolls. Or, if you're not wanting to eat just yet..." He took a step into the bathroom.

Teresa rolled her eyes to look past him, at the closet door, which was sliding open. James didn't see it.

Then things happened very, very fast.

Lou came out of the closet with his steel hook swinging at James's neck. The paralysis in Teresa's mouth finally broke and she screamed. But almost before Lou moved, before Teresa had made a sound, James was spinning around. He dropped the bag of Chinese takeout but kept his grip on the neck of the bottle. The bottle met the hook with a crash. Glass shattered and wine sprayed in all directions.

Lou kept coming, grabbing James's wrist in his left hand. The force of his rush flung James into the bathroom. The small, cramped space was suddenly full of flailing limbs. James tried to jab at Lou with the broken neck of the bottle, but his wrist was held tight by the bigger, stronger man. He punched Lou in the stomach with his off hand, which didn't seem to have any effect. Lou swung the hook again.

James turned his head sharply at the last moment. Instead of piercing his eye, the tip of the hook dug a furrow along the side of his scalp. With a sort of detached horror Teresa saw three big, fat drops of blood fall into the bathwater, beginning to diffuse into it and tint the water pink. James stumbled, his wrist still gripped tightly by his opponent. Lou swept the hook up high, ready to bring it down into James's face.

She wasn't angry. There was no room in her head for anything but fear. She was still so frightened she felt like throwing up. But Teresa did the only thing she could think to do. She cupped her hands and flung a double handful of bathwater into Lou's face.

It didn't hurt him a bit. But it did distract and blind him for a crucial fraction of a second.

James was still moving. His right wrist was held tight, but his left hand was free. That hand dove into his hip pocket and came out with something small and shiny. With a flick of his wrist, he opened a folding knife and slashed into Lou's forearm. The Sicilian fell back with a startled cry, a bright line of blood showing on his arm. James shoved off from the back wall and wrenched his other hand free. He snapped his right hand in a quick motion and his fighting knife dropped into it from its hidden clip. The Scarab tactical knife shone like liquid silver.

For a moment the two men faced each other, both bleeding. Lou held his hook, poised and ready, its tip bloody. James had a knife in each hand.

"Evening, Lou," James said in a deceptively light, pleasant voice. "Been a while."

"Corky," Lou said, copying his tone. A drop of James's blood dripped from the hook and spattered on the bathroom tiles.

"Only my friends call me that," James replied.

"We go back far enough," Lou said.

"As a matter of curiosity, how'd you find me?"

"Got your license plate at the restaurant, called a guy I know in El Paso."

"How'd you know I was going to El Paso?"

Lou smiled. "You'd hardly be headed for New Orleans after your last visit. Even you aren't that reckless. Especially with a girl to look out for."

"The lass has nothing to do with this," James said. "This is about you and me."

"I couldn't agree more," Lou said. He slowly flexed the hand holding the hook. "But you're the one who brought her along."

"We should talk about that," James said. "See, I made a promise to look after her."

"Don't write checks you can't cash," Lou said.

The two men had hardly moved while they were talking, but Teresa could see their tense muscles and the way they watched each other. They were fighting while standing still, both probing for any opening, any weakness.

"I guess I've no choice but to kill you, then," James said.

"Like you did to my brother? Whenever you're ready, you mick son of a bitch," Lou said, and for the first time, he sounded less than pleasant.

At that moment there was a sharp knock at the room's outer door. All three of them flinched in surprise. A female voice called from the hallway.

"Ma'am? Are you all right?"

Someone had heard Teresa's scream. "Call 911!" she shouted. Then things happened fast again.

"Don't!" James said sharply. Lou made a sudden, sweeping swing at James with his hook. James, still holding his little pocketknife in his left hand and his Scarab in his right, crouched and stabbed, but the bathroom floor was covered with water and wine. His foot slipped and he went sideways, cracking his knee against the bathtub. The slip spoiled his lunge, but it also made Lou's swing miss just over his head. The hook whistled and tore into the shower curtain. It snagged there for a second.

Lou cursed in Italian and yanked on the hook. James, recovering from his slip, coiled his feet underneath himself. Teresa grabbed the shower curtain and hung on for dear life. Lou gave a savage tug, and the curtain slipped in Teresa's wet hands, but she kept her desperate grip on her end. Then Lou, seeing James coming back up, let go of his weapon and sprang back out of the bathroom.

James had hurt his leg in his fall, but his hands were as fast as ever. The Scarab stabbed up.

Lou twisted away from the blade. It gouged into his side, cutting flesh with astonishing ease. As the Sicilian stumbled away, he caught the bathroom door with one hand and jerked it shut, slamming it closed.

James didn't hesitate. He dropped his pocketknife and snatched open the door again, just in time to hear a startled cry from the woman in the hallway. Lou was already out the main door. James went after him. On his second running stride, his leg buckled. He hissed in pain and fell again, bracing himself against the wall.

Teresa was feeling decidedly shaky herself. But she knew she couldn't let herself give in to the weakness. James had saved her. Now it was time for her to help him. He was hurt, she didn't know how badly, and Lou was still out there. He'd be back. She stood up in the tub. Ignoring the water that cascaded off her, ignoring her own nakedness, she stepped out of the tub, nearly losing her own footing on the slick bathroom tiles. The room was a mess of water, spilled wine, broken glass, and blood. She went to the outside door in two careful strides, managing to avoid stepping on any of the glass, and slammed it, flipping the deadbolt.

"Good lass," James said through clenched teeth. "Get dressed, quick as you can. We'd best be leaving."

Teresa nodded, already on her way to her bag. She grabbed a T-shirt, underwear, and jeans and threw them on in record time. The clothes immediately soaked up the water from her body, but she hardly noticed. She felt light-headed and disconnected from herself. Not bothering with socks, she slipped her feet into her shoes.

"Where are we going?" she asked, marveling at how calm and collected she sounded now.

"Out the window," James said. "We don't want to meet Lou in the hallway."

"We're on the second floor," she reminded him.

"Doesn't matter," he said. "We can make the jump. It's only ten feet. Just grab the sill and let yourself drop."

"But your leg's hurt."

"Never mind that," he said with an attempt at his usual carefree smile. It wasn't entirely convincing. "Here's the keys. I parked in the second row, just to the left of the front door." He handed her the car keys. "I can't run on this bloody leg, so you'll have to fetch the car. Once you're on the ground, Terry, run. Run like the very devil was after you. Don't waste time looking for Lou. Assume he'll see you. Start the car, drive as close to the window as you can, and stop, but leave it running. I'll be waiting."

"Why don't we wait for the police?" she asked.

"They'll take ten minutes getting here. We could be dead in five."

She nodded. Then, in spite of her resolve, she felt her lip tremble. His face softened. He leaned in and kissed her cheek.

"There's my brave lass," he said. "No time to waste. You can do this."

He unlatched the window and slid it open. The dry desert air, still holding the heat of the day, wafted into the room. Teresa took a deep breath. Then she swung a leg over the windowsill, took a firm grip, and let herself drop.

James was right; it was only a few feet to the ground, and didn't hurt. She bent her knees to cushion the impact, and then she was up and running for the parking lot. As he'd instructed her, she looked neither left nor right. Teresa was in fairly good shape for a schoolteacher in her thirties, but she was no sprinter. The hot Arizona wind clawed its way down her dry throat. She fixed her eyes on the familiar shape of the Accord and got the keys ready in her right hand.

It seemed to take endless minutes to cover the ground, but was really probably more like twenty seconds. She pushed the unlocking button on the key fob when she was five yards away and heard the welcoming chirp in response. Then she was there, scrabbling at the door handle. With a dry sob of relief, she clawed the door open and flung herself into the driver's seat. She rammed the key into the ignition and cranked it hard. In a horror movie, the car wouldn't have started, and she somehow expected that. But the Honda was in good working order. Its engine roared immediately to life. She put it in gear and stomped the accelerator.

Teresa didn't own a car. She hadn't driven in years. But like riding a bike, it was something you didn't forget how to do. She was unfamiliar with this vehicle's layout and steering, and the seat wasn't in the right place for her height, but considering the other things she'd had to do on this trip, it was nothing to worry about. As she drove back the way she'd come, she saw James pitch their luggage out the window. He let himself down after it. When he landed, his leg crumpled and he fell, catching himself on his hands. Teresa winced in sympathy. Then she was there.

She hit the brakes. He limped the few feet to the curbside, holding their bags in both hands. Teresa reached across for the passenger door, momentarily thankful she hadn't bothered with her seatbelt, and got his door open. He pitched the bags between the headrests into the back and flopped into the passenger seat.

"Go," he gasped.

At that moment the front and back windshields both cracked, spider-webs of safety glass spreading out from small, neat holes. Simultaneously, there was a series of popping sounds. Teresa blinked in surprise.

"Go!" James said again, more urgently. Two more pops sounded and the back windshield shattered completely.

Teresa realized then that they were being shot at. She tried to push the gas pedal through the floor. Tires shrieked. The Accord lurched as one front wheel went onto the curb. She swerved back onto the pavement as a horrible burnt-rubber smell hit her nose. The entrance to the hotel parking lot was behind them. A glance in the rearview mirror showed Lou, standing in the parking lot, pointing a pistol at them. Even as she looked, he fired again. The bullet punched into their rear fender. Without thinking about it, Teresa twisted the steering wheel hard to the right. There wasn't an access point, just a few feet of gravel between the parking lot and Corona Road. She aimed between a couple of ornamental shrubs and jumped the curb. Gravel flew. The car lurched and bounced. They landed on pavement again with another squeal of tires. Fortunately, traffic wasn't heavy on the road at that time of evening. She angled east and laid on some speed, leaving Lou receding behind them out of sight.

"Turn right," James snapped. "Into the airport economy lot."

"But... we need to get away," she protested.

"And we will," he said. "But he knows this car. And we'd not get far on a highway in this condition. We look like we've been to war. We're pretty bloody conspicuous. We need to change rides."

"Right," she said. "Change rides." She forced herself to slow down, though every nerve in her body wanted to go faster, to leave that horrible man as far behind them as possible. She turned into the airport parking area and slowed to parking lot speed, which felt basically like standing still to her overcharged nervous system.

James was looking out at the rows of parked cars. "There," he said, pointing. "Take that place."

She obediently parked; a clumsy, badly-angled job that showed her rustiness behind the wheel. "Now what do we do?" she asked.

He reached back for his duffel. "Get your things," he said. "I'll not be but a moment." Then he got out of the car, moving gingerly on his injured leg, and extracted a long strip of metal from the bag. Before she quite realized what he was doing, he'd gone to the car next to theirs, a beige Toyota Camry, and slipped the metal thing down into the door panel. A quick wiggle and upward jerk later, the door was unlocked. James opened the door and bent under the dashboard, snatching a screwdriver out of his bag of tricks. He did something with the steering column, and a few seconds after that, the Camry's engine started. He straightened up.

"Let's go, love."

Numbly, Teresa picked up her bag of meager belongings and went around the front of their car. James unlocked the Camry's passenger door for her and she climbed in. Then, he drove out of the parking lot like he'd just done the most natural thing in the world. He turned east on Corona again. Behind them, Teresa heard sirens and saw flashing police lights at the hotel, but James didn't stop or turn back. He worked his way east and north, back to the Interstate. Soon they were back on I-10, headed northwest into the last glow of the sunset.

*   *   *

"We had an... accident," Teresa explained to Norma. "On the road. James was hurt, a little. It frightened me."

"Oh, you poor dear," Norma said. "I was in a car accident a few years ago. A drunk driver ran a red light and just slammed right into us. It's one of the scariest things I can remember. I do hope your young man was all right."

Teresa nodded. "It wasn't too bad, I suppose. The fear was the worst part of it."

"God looks out for us," Norma said.

Teresa nodded again, unconvinced. She was a good, churchgoing woman, but she no longer believed bad things couldn't happen to good people.

"It was difficult," she said. "It made some changes in our plans."

"Plans are like that," the older woman said. "It's best not to get too attached to them."

Chapter 10

"James?" Teresa finally said.

"Aye?"

"You just stole a car."

He nodded. "Aye, that's so."

"Is that... okay?"

"We'll keep it only so long as we must," he said. "We'll leave it up the road. They'll get it back, with only a wee bit of inconvenience. If you'd like, I'll even fill the tank before we dump it."

"And then what? Steal another?"

"I'll make arrangements," he said sharply. "Now will you let me think for a moment?"

Teresa flinched. "I'm... I'm sorry," she said, forcing the words out of trembling lips. Then she started sobbing, her entire body shaking, tears spilling out of her eyes and rolling down her cheeks.

"Hey," he said. "Hey, Terry, it's all right. It's all right, love. You're grand. Everything's fine. I shouldn't have nipped your head off. It's me should be apologizing."

Teresa buried her face in her hands. "I'm sorry," she said again, and she wasn't sure what she was apologizing for. It might be for panicking, for not fighting harder against Fishhook Lou, for breaking down in tears, or maybe all of the above. Mostly, now that the immediate danger was past, she just needed to let out some of the fear and anxiety that was filling her to bursting.

"Sweet Jesus, love," James said. "It's me left you there, all alone. It's me didn't realize Lou made us. Christ on His bloody cross, I shouldn't have gone through Louisiana in the first place! But Terry, there's plenty of time to be beating the shite out of ourselves for our sins once we're out of the hot water. Right now I'm needing to know exactly what happened back there, before I turned up. I need you to tell me. It's important. Can you do that, love?"

She sniffled and wiped at her eyes with the already-damp sleeve of her T-shirt. "Okay," she managed. Then, hesitantly, she forced herself to describe Lou's arrival. As she spoke, she saw James gripping the steering wheel so hard his knuckles were trembling. But he didn't say anything, except to ask her to elaborate on a couple of points.

"So he didn't recognize you?" James asked, after she told how she'd made up a name on the spot.

"I don't think so," she said. "He wasn't after me."

"Nay," he said grimly. "He was hunting me. Some bloody guardian I've turned out to be."

"I should have warned you," she said. "When you came in."

Now he looked surprised. "You did warn me," he said. "It was all over your face, Terry. You might as well have screamed there was another lad in the place. You should've seen your eyes, love. Like bloody great saucers, they were."

"I was so scared," she whispered. "If he'd... if he'd killed you, would he have let me go?"

"Are you really wanting to know that, love?" he asked.

She nodded.

"You'd seen his face. You knew his name. He'd hardly have left you as a witness," James said quietly. "You know that."

Teresa nodded again. She shuddered, remembering those flat, black, hard eyes and the way he'd talked about his grandparents, and then about poking out her eyes, in the exact same tone of voice. "What's the matter with him?" she asked, still in a near-whisper.

James shrugged. "Lads like that come in two varieties," he said. "There's ordinary thugs, who are just lads who don't mind hurting someone for money. And then there's the sort that take pleasure in the hurting and the killing. Lou's one of the latter sort. I imagine if he wasn't a Mafia associate, he'd be off on his own doing pretty much the same thing. A serial killer or the like."

"What happened between the two of you? Why does he hate you so much?"

He shook his head. "That's ancient history."

"Not for him."

"That's a fair point." James sighed. "Lou Andreotti... well, I cost him a great deal of money a few years back. I helped seize a shipment of goods his people were moving into New Orleans. It was arms, machine guns and the like. Some other lads and I got a tip, and we got our hands on them before Lou could take delivery. There was a bit of a scuffle, and two of his lads copped it."

"Copped it?"

"They ended up face down in the Gulf, drifting with the tide."

"Oh."

"One of them was a scunner called Benny Andreotti. Lou's younger brother, I'm sorry to say."

"Oh," she said again. "Does he blame you?"

He nodded.

"Did... did you...?" she started, but couldn't quite finish.

"He thinks I did," James said. "Nothing else matters much."

Teresa shivered as a sudden chill seized her. James noticed it. "Here's me apologizing again," he said, quickly reaching for the air-conditioning knob on the dashboard. "And here's you wearing wet clothes, wet hair down your neck, and I'm freezing your bloody toes off. Terry, you've got to take care of yourself. If you're cold, you have to tell me."

"You're taking care of me," she said softly.

"And a piss-poor job I've done of it tonight," he muttered. He angled the Camry into the exit lane. "We've gone far enough. We don't want to be leaving town in this car." He took a left under the Interstate onto St Mary's Road. "We'll just pick up some medical supplies and change transport, and then we'll be on our way."

Teresa saw the blue H sign that indicated a hospital. "Oh, God," she said, suddenly remembering. "You're hurt!"

"I'll live," he said. "I've taken plenty worse than this."

"I'm sure the doctor will fix you up," she agreed, trying to be upbeat.

"No doctor," he said. "And no hospital."

"But..." she said, pointing. The hospital was just ahead, on their left, its entrance shining with bright floodlights in the near-dark. Those lights promised warmth, shelter, safety.

"Nay," he said. "Lou knows I've been hurt. He might have lads looking for me there. And it's possible the coppers will be checking the hospitals, too. We left something of a mess in that room." He turned right just before the hospital and drove into the parking lot of a pharmacy.

"James," she said, "why don't you want to get help from the local police? Surely they'd help us. I know they're not from the NYPD, but they're still cops!"

"Terry, you'll have to go in," he said, sliding the Camry into a parking space. "I can't walk so well at the moment, and I'm afraid my face might attract attention. You'll need surgical thread, a suture kit, some sterile gauze, a bottle of disinfectant... nay, never mind the disinfectant. And a bottle of the strongest pain medicine you can get over the counter, without showing identification. Here's two hundred dollars. If you're wanting anything for your own comfort, get that, too. I'll be needing something to keep me awake, so buy a half-dozen bottles of something full of caffeine. And some food, whatever you'd like, as long as it's something we can eat in the car. Be as quick as you can, love."

She nodded and got out of the car, her question unanswered. Holding the roll of twenties he'd given her, she went into the pharmacy. Feeling like she was half-asleep and wandering through some sort of strange fever dream, she walked up and down the aisles, picking out the things he'd told her to get. Even though they'd skipped supper, she wasn't the least bit hungry. She grabbed a few bags of chips off the shelf, hardly looking at them, and added a six-pack of cola. As an afterthought, she got a packet of Slim Jims for protein and a bottle of lemonade.

"Evening, ma'am," said the lady behind the counter. "Are you a Rewards member?"

Teresa blinked at her. "What?"

"A Rewards member," the woman repeated, pointing to the keypad. Then she looked closer at her. "Ma'am? Are you all right?"

Teresa nodded slowly. "Yes," she said, realizing only then how she must look. Her hair, still damp, was a tangled mess.

Her eyes were puffy from crying, and she was wearing a thin T-shirt that was wet most of the way through. She was probably giving anyone who looked at her a good show, she realized. On any other day of her life, she would have been mortified. Now, it hardly seemed to matter.

"Listen, ma'am," the woman said. "If you're in some sort of trouble, I can help you." She looked outside, where the Camry was visible, James's silhouette behind the steering wheel. "I can call the police."

Teresa thought how James might have handled the situation and made herself smile. "No," she said, trying to make her voice lighter than she felt. "That's fine. My... my boyfriend and I just needed to pick up some things. He had a little accident, cut himself in the bathroom." She indicated the first-aid supplies. "I was in the shower. We're fine."

The woman nodded and relaxed a little. "The hospital's just down the way," she said.

"It's not that bad," Teresa said. "Really."

"Okay, ma'am. There's your total."

Teresa peeled off some bills and handed them over. She'd miscounted, and needed another twenty to make up the difference. As the woman counted out her change, Teresa stared at the coins on the countertop. The numbers wouldn't add up in her head.

"I hope he's okay," the clerk said. "Your receipt's in the bag."

"Thanks," Teresa said and went back to the car, feeling the other woman's curious stare on her back.

"We've an auto part store just up the way," James said as she climbed into the car. "With a filling station and garage across from it. We can change rides there. That's if you're not wanting me to steal another one."

"I'd rather you didn't," she said.

James drove around back of the gas station and parked in an open space. "You just stay here," he said. "I'll take care of things." He got out of the car and limped to the garage, his leg dragging badly. It was closed for the night, but the gas station out front was still brightly lit. Teresa watched, hardly able to believe her eyes, as James calmly picked the lock and went into the maintenance area as if he didn't have a care in the world. After a few minutes, he came back out, twirling a ring of keys. He hobbled to a Honda CRV parked nearby and waved her over. She picked up their things and crossed the asphalt to meet him. He got carefully in, adjusted the seat, and started the engine.

"Grand," he said.

Teresa climbed into the passenger seat, stowing their luggage in the back. "I thought you weren't going to steal another car," she said.

"I'm not," he said, looking offended. "I've bought this one."

"You were carrying enough money to *buy a car?*" she exclaimed.

"Not precisely," he said. "I left the proprietor a note, with a telephone number he can call. The lad who answers will provide him with a reasonable sum. He'll do all right out of this."

"That doesn't sound like something the NYPD would do," she said. But as she said it, she was trying to get a closer look at the left side of James's face. It had looked funny, even half-hidden in the shadows. "What's that on your cheek?"

"What?" he asked, putting a hand up. "Oh, that? It's just blood, nothing to fret over."

Then Teresa remembered the way Lou's hook had gouged the side of his head. "I'd better take a look at it," she said.

"Not here," he said, putting the car in gear. "See up ahead? There's a golf course. No lads will be golfing this time of night. We'll stop there and I'll let us into the country club. There'll be a washroom we can use."

At this point, after all the crazy things that had happened, Teresa just went with it. The idea of breaking into a golf clubhouse didn't seem all that strange or even exciting anymore. She nodded.

"Okay."

*   *   *

The lock on the country club's front door was no more challenging for James than the car door had been. They were inside in less than a minute. He led the way to the women's restroom, went inside, and flipped on the lights. The bright, cold fluorescents made everything suddenly sharp and clear. The blood on James's face looked almost black under the bluish light. It was on his hands, on his shirt, everywhere.

"Not to fear, love," he said. "It's not half so bad as it looks." He glanced in the mirror. "Lay out our medical things on the changing table there."

"What are you going to do?" she asked.

He probed the gash with his fingertips. "I'll sew it up, naturally. You didn't think I'd leave my brains exposed to the Arizona desert, did you?"

"James! Your brain is not exposed!"

He squinted at the mirror. "I could have sworn I saw something gray and squishy..."

"Stop it this minute," she said, reverting to her schoolteacher's voice. "I'll do the sewing. I don't think you know what you're doing with a needle and thread."

"I once stitched up a lad's belly with dental floss and a knitting needle," he said.

"Even if that's true, it wasn't your own belly," she retorted. As she spoke, she picked up the suturing needle. It was already attached to the thread, she saw, and the needle was an unusual shape. It was curved like... like a fishhook, she saw with an inward shudder. But she knew perfectly well how to sew. Her mother had taught her to mend her own clothing. And this wouldn't be the first gash she'd tended. A grade-school teacher had to deal with bumps, scrapes, and skinned knees on a regular basis.

"Wash it out," she instructed. "Then we need to disinfect it. Why didn't you have me get some antiseptic?"

He bent over the sink and splashed water onto his face. Drops of blood spattered the base of the mirror and the sink. "I've a bottle already about me."

When he had cleaned the wound as well as he could, he reached into his hip pocket and took out his flask of whiskey. Unscrewing the cap, he tilted his head and poured a generous splash of hard liquor onto his temple. He sucked in a sharp gasp and held perfectly still for a moment. Then he raised the flask to his lips and took a big swallow.

"Are you all right?" she asked.

He smiled, and it looked genuine for the first time since Lou had attacked him. "I'm right as rain, love. Though I think whiskey's best taken by mouth, rather than straight through the skin. I'm ready now. Are you needing a taste to steady your hands?"

"James, I'm not going to get drunk before stitching up your head," she said. "None of the girls will like you if you have a zigzag scar all down your face."

He laughed. "What do you mean, love? Every lass likes a lad with a scar or two. It's like a Persian rug. The imperfection makes you notice the beauty all the more."

"Is that so?" she said dryly. As she started stitching up the gash, she marveled at how easily they had fallen back into their familiar rhythm, in spite of the horrible things that had happened and nearly happened. She kept the stitches small, neat, and close together. James was tough. He didn't twitch a muscle as the needle pierced his skin. He was actually humming a soft tune while she worked.

"Why didn't he shoot me on the way to the car?" she wondered aloud. "Or shoot you in the room."

"Lou doesn't care for guns," James said. "I'm surprised he had one with him. I'd imagine it was in his car and he had to run out to fetch it. Fortunately, he's an even worse shot than I am."

"Is that why you prefer to use a knife?" she asked.

"Aye. Also, a knife can be used for any number of things. A gun's really only practical for threatening a lad, or for shooting him." He sighed. "I should have had him in the washroom. I must be getting clumsy in my old age."

"The floor was slippery," she said. "I almost fell, too. How's your leg?"

"I wrenched my knee," he said. "I think I'll be all right, but I'd best not be running for a few days. You needn't fret, love. All my other mechanics are working fine." He winked at her reflection in the mirror.

"James! I can't believe you're thinking about... that at a time like this."

"No better time," he said cheerfully. "There's nothing quite like riding the feeling that comes from cheating death. It's an experience like none other."

She shook her head. "You're absolutely incorrigible. But thank you."

"For what?"

"For saving my life."

His eyes narrowed, and he would have shaken his head if she hadn't been stitching him together. "Nay, love. I'm the one put you in danger in the first place."

"It wasn't your fault."

"Nor yours."

"How did he get through the lock on our hotel room?"

James shrugged. "There's ways through just about any lock."

"You know a lot about being a criminal."

"I've associated with a great many felons over the years," he said. "I've kept my eyes open and picked up some things along the way."

"When did you stitch that guy together with dental floss?"

"Oh, that was back in Ireland," he said. "During the Troubles. A lad I was with caught a bullet in his middle. I had to fish it out and patch him together. It's a grand story, but perhaps one for another time."

"James?"

"Aye?"

"Why did we run away from the police?"

"What do you mean?"

"You shouted 'don't' when I told the hotel lady to call the police. Then you avoided them. Why?"

He looked at her. "Terry, we're traveling incognito, under false names with unofficial identification. They'd only be doing their job if they arrested the both of us."

"But at least we'd be safe."

"For how long? Your life depends on people thinking you're dead. Once they establish your identity, the whole thing's for nothing."

Teresa nodded her understanding. She finished stitching and tied off the thread. "How's that?" she asked.

He cocked his head and examined her handiwork in the mirror. "Grand," he said. "I'll keep for a while. Now, there's just one more thing." He unbuckled his belt and unzipped his trousers.

"James!" she exclaimed. "Not here!"

He grinned. "For once, that's not the first thing on my mind, love." He carefully eased his pants down to his ankles and looked at his injured leg.

"Oh my God," Teresa said, putting a hand to her mouth. James's right knee was horribly swollen and discolored. "What happened?"

He gently probed the area around the knee and winced. "Nothing too terrible, I think. Just dislocated the kneecap."

"That's serious," she said. "We need to take you to a doctor."

"I said no doctors, Terry," he said. He studied the injury and gingerly probed it. "I saw a lad with this condition during a game of rugby, once. There was a doctor at the match and he simply popped it back into place. The lad sat on the sidelines a few minutes, then finished the game. You Americans would probably have wanted him to rest for six weeks or some such nonsense. Perhaps that's why rugger's never caught on the same way on this side of the pond."

"You can't mean you're going to..." she began.

"And why not?" he replied. "How hard can it be?" He leaned against the wall. Before she could say or do anything, he reached for the kneecap and gave a sharp push and twist. "Jesus Christ!"

Teresa wasn't nearly as quick as James. Her desperate lunge was only just in time to keep his head from hitting the floor as he crumpled. They went down together onto the cold tile in a tangle, James as white as a sheet.

"James?" she murmured after a long moment. He was lying half on top of her, completely limp. Then, louder, fighting down panic, "James!"

He groaned. "Sweet mother of God," he mumbled.

Teresa started crying again, in relief this time. "Are you okay?" she managed to ask.

"I'm grand. Never better. The nuns would swat me for swearing like that." He tried to sit up and failed. He tried again and, with Teresa's help, braced his back against the wall.

"James, don't you ever do that again," she said, trying unsuccessfully to keep the tremor out of her voice. "Don't you dare."

"Well, love, it wasn't exactly the most enjoyable experience," he said. "And since you feel so strongly on the subject, I'll avoid it in the future."

"And your leg?" she ventured, looking down at it.

He made a small, experimental movement. Then he flexed the knee more widely. "Aye, it'll do," he said. "Still a bit sore, but nothing I can't handle. Just a wee nip and I'll be grand." He took a slug of whiskey and made as if to stand up.

"No, you don't!" she exclaimed. "Let me help you." She got up and offered her hands. He reached for her and she helped him to his feet. He put a little experimental weight on his right leg, then more.

"I'm all right, really," he said. "Christ, this is bloody embarrassing." He was still limping a little, but could walk almost normally.

"Okay," she said. "But you really should rest it. I'll drive."

"Are you sure? You've had a terrible shock, love."

"At least I haven't been bleeding and messing around with my own bones and passing out on the floor," she said. "Not to mention swigging whiskey straight from the bottle. If you try to drive in your condition, we'll get pulled over by the highway patrol. How far are we going tonight?"

"Out of Tucson," he said. "I'm thinking we'd best make Phoenix before we stop. It's just a couple hours up the road. Then we'll find a place to get some sleep. I'm thinking we're in need of it."

＊　　＊　　＊

Teresa experienced that nighttime drive through the desert as if it was a dream. The CRV's tires hummed on the asphalt. The empty space on all sides was eerie to her city-bred eyes. It felt like they were the only people on Earth. James, in the passenger seat, was quieter than he'd been at any point on their journey. She risked a glance at him half an hour outside Tucson and saw his eyes were closed. She let him sleep. In some ways, he'd had a harder evening than she had.

Driving on a dark road with a sleeping passenger was one of the loneliest things she'd ever done. The desert highway might have been on the far side of the world, or maybe on some other world altogether. The hum of the tires on the blacktop was a hypnotic drone. An immense weariness oozed into her brain, weighing down her eyelids.

Fishhook Lou grabbed her by the hair and pressed the tip of his cargo hook into her throat, just below her chin.

Teresa's eyes snapped open and she gasped. The car had drifted over the center line. Heart pounding, wide awake now, she blinked repeatedly and stared into the night. She gripped the steering wheel with shaking hands and wondered just how much adrenaline the human body could produce. She was still tired, but there was no chance at all she'd go back to sleep anytime soon.

Interstate 10 came up on Phoenix from the south. On the outskirts, Teresa saw signs for hotels. It looked like they had a choice between a Best Western and a hotel/casino called the Wild Horse Pass. She smiled, thinking she could guess which one James would recommend. And what was the worst thing that could happen? Someone had already tried to kill them that night. She took the exit and aimed for the Wild Horse Pass's parking lot.

She parked and shut off the motor. James didn't react. His eyes were still closed, his breathing slow and regular.

"James," she said quietly.

Nothing.

"We're here," she tried.

Still no response.

Teresa unbuckled her seat belt and gently shook his shoulder. He mumbled something unintelligible.

"James Corcoran," she said in her best schoolteacher tone. "Wake up."

"Why?" he asked without opening his eyes.

"Because it's time for bed," she replied.

"Love, that makes no sense at all," he said, but he sat up and looked at her. In the parking lot lights, she could see his eyes were suddenly bright and alert. "Where are we?"

"The Wild Horse Pass Hotel," she said, then added, "and casino. Phoenix."

"Any trouble?"

She shook her head.

"Grand." James opened the passenger door. Before she could stop him or say anything, he put his feet down on the asphalt. He winced and almost fell over, catching himself on the door.

"Your leg," she said unnecessarily.

"Most of it, at any rate," he said ruefully. "You needn't fret, love. I'm grand. It just slipped my mind for a moment."

"Should we go in and get a room?" she asked.

"In a moment," he said, opening the back door of the CRV and pulling a screwdriver out of his bag of tricks. "There's one thing to see to first. Keep an eye out for witnesses, aye?"

"Witnesses?" she echoed, not really understanding. But James was already in action, carefully bending over the car next to theirs. In a matter of moments, he'd switched their license plates with those of the stranger. Teresa wondered what sort of security cameras the hotel had, but figured the casino guards were probably paying more attention to what was going on at the game tables. The parking lot was full of cars, but no one passed near them while James committed his most recent vehicular crime.

"All's well now," he said, straightening up with a smile. "Let's be on our way."

Teresa could only shake her head. "James, I'm glad I didn't have you in one of my classrooms. I bet you were a terror when you were a boy."

"The penguins did rap my knuckles once or twice," he admitted. "I could tell you some stories, but you'd only think the less of me."

This was definitely a swanky place. Teresa was glad she wasn't paying for it. The lobby of the hotel was a tall, round room with a statue of a leaping horse directly beneath an enormous chandelier. The glass construction reminded her of the world's largest icicle. It seemed like a strange decoration for a hotel in Arizona, but her capacity of surprise was just about exhausted. James limped to the front desk and paid for their room. Then they rode the elevator to the top floor.

"Penthouse?" she asked.

"Naturally." He leaned against the elevator wall to rest his injured knee.

"James?"

"Aye?"

"Where's all this money coming from?"

"Personal vacation fund." His eyes were closed. He looked very tired.

"You stole that car's license plates."

"And a whole other car earlier tonight," he agreed.

"What kind of cop are you?"

"What do you think I am?"

She shook her head. "I don't know what to think. Let's just get a door between us and... and everything."

The room was fancier than the one they'd left behind in Tucson, including a king-size bed and a nice window view of the hotel's swimming pool. They dropped their bags in the corner. Teresa sank down onto the bed.

"God," she said. "What time is it?"

"It's early yet," he said. "Not even eleven."

"Really?" The evening felt like it had taken years.

He smiled and sat down beside her. "Aye. Are you hungry? We missed dinner."

"Not really."

"Are you wanting a shower, then?"

Teresa shuddered. "No."

Recognition came into his eyes. "I'm sorry, love. That's right careless of me to mention."

"It's okay," she said. "I... I just don't know what... What do we do now?"

"What do you mean?"

"He... that man... he was going to kill us. Both of us."

James nodded. "But he didn't."

"You almost died."

He grinned. "You know what another word is for almost dying, love? Living. And that's what we're doing. Living."

"It's not that simple." She had her arms wrapped around herself, holding her own elbows.

"Of course it is," James said. He slid closer to her and put an arm around her shoulders. She instinctively nestled against the comforting warmth of his body.

"James?"

"Aye?"

"Hold me."

So he held her, and she cried a little. She couldn't help it, even though she didn't even know what she was crying about. Residual fear, relief, stress, all of it was blended together. But James was there with her, real and alive, and they were safe, at least for a little while, and that was the important thing. He kissed her forehead, then both cheeks, his lips brushing away the trails of her tears.

"There's my brave lass," he murmured. "You did save my life, you know."

"I did not," she said.

"Of course you did. Twice over. You warned me, and you disarmed the lad."

"I'm no hero, James."

He smiled. "You needn't be a victim, either. Terry, we're alive. And your life is yours, love. Be proud of it."

"You call me that a lot."

"What's that?"

"Love."

His smile slipped a little on one side. "Ah, that's just my way of talking."

"Is it?" She put up a hand to his face, careful not to touch the fresh stitches.

"I warned you about me, Terry," he said quietly.

"You did," she agreed. "You said you'd break my heart."

"I will."

"No you won't."

"You don't know that."

She drew him closer. "I do."

"Terry..." he began. Their eyes were only inches apart.

"Tell me you don't love me," she said.

"What?"

"I dare you," Teresa said. "Look me in the eye and tell me that."

Now he looked confused. "Why on Earth would you be asking me that?"

"I don't think you can lie to me," she said. "So look at me and tell me you don't love me."

"You're the one playing games now," he said, his smile returning. "I don't think you're much of a card player, so let me give you a bit of advice. When you've a losing hand, you either bluff and raise, or you toss in your cards. You don't call the bet."

"James? What on earth are you talking about?"

He bent toward her and kissed her. It wasn't a soft, comforting kiss like he'd put on her cheeks. It was hot, urgent, passionate. The sudden intensity of it stole the breath out of her mouth in a startled gasp. His lips crushed against hers. Teresa was astonished at the fierce heat that rushed through her body at the contact. She'd been weak, tired, and frightened a moment before. Now she understood, in a flash of sensual insight, what he'd meant when he talked about riding the feeling of cheating death. Her nerve endings caught fire all over her body. She opened her mouth and moaned, tasting him. For a moment she worried about his injuries, about hurting him more, but a second later she forgot all about that. They tumbled down onto the comforter, pulling at each other's clothes, hungrily feasting on the sheer intoxicating feeling of being alive.

* * *

"Ladies and gentlemen, we are beginning our descent into JFK Airport. Please fasten your seatbelts, and ensure your seat backs are in the upright position."

Teresa looked out the airplane's window. There was New York, the city she'd never really meant to leave. Now, coming back, it didn't feel like coming home. It felt like stepping into a lion's den. Something sharp poked the palms of her hands. She looked down at her hands and saw they were clenched into fists, her nails digging into her own skin.

James was down there, she reminded herself. He needed her, and he was her home now. It was a stupid idea, she knew it. Detective O'Reilly would have been horrified if she knew. But what could she do? She should never have let him leave, should have made him stay with her. They should have stayed in Mexico, even after what happened there.

Chapter 11

Teresa was worried about James the following morning. But he claimed to be feeling fine, and though he walked with a slight limp, he didn't seem much worse for wear.

"Touch of a good lass," he said with a grin. "Cures all manner of ailments. I feel like a new man." He leaned in and kissed her.

After a leisurely breakfast, they got on the road, rejoining their old friend Interstate 10. James was driving again, claiming his knee was practically as good as new. They made excellent time on the desert road, and after a few miles James took the Highway 85 exit. They drove south for half an hour, until 85 spat them out onto Interstate 8. Then it was a straight shot west, through Yuma and several smaller towns, over the California state line to San Diego. The driving time added up to about five and a half hours. Compared to the previous days of the sitting in cars, Teresa felt like it was just a short jaunt up the road.

"Lou won't find us again, will he?" she finally asked, trying not to sound anxious about it.

"Don't see how he could, love," James said, giving her a quick smile. "We've changed cars, so he'd hardly know our ride, and we're well clear of him."

"He caught us once before. You said he wouldn't."

"There's other things the Fishhook has to worry about," he said. "The coppers in Tucson will be looking for him, if they've not caught him already."

"That's true," she said, somewhat reassured. "He really hates you, doesn't he?"

"Aye."

"I don't know how anyone could hate you. Even with what happened to his brother."

"Well, lass, you've only known me these few days. I assure you, I've made my share of enemies. Besides, think of yourself. You're a right charming colleen, love, and there's lads would kill you if they'd the chance. Else why would we be doing what we're doing?"

She nodded, but she was thinking, and thinking hard. "James?"

"Aye?"

"Why did you become a cop?"

"Is that important?"

She looked at his face. He was watching the road. "It's important to me," she said.

He took a deep breath. "Are you sure you're wanting to know about me? My past? All of it?"

She put a hand on his leg, careful to choose the uninjured one. "James, it's not like we haven't been... close. I'm not afraid of you. You can tell me anything."

He gave a short sound that was almost too bitter to be a laugh. "You say that because I've not told you yet."

Teresa left her hand on his leg. "James, I know there's things you don't like about yourself. You... you don't think you're good for women, even though you're good at talking to them. And more than talking, I guess. I think part of you hates yourself. But I don't hate you, James. I love you."

He flinched. "Terry, don't. Please, don't."

She didn't relent. "Trust me, James. You've saved my life. You've protected me, you've been good to me. I trust you. There's nothing you could say to change that." She hesitated. "I mean, you're not going to tell me you're married, are you?"

He laughed, sounding more like himself. "Nay, love. Never once in my life, no matter how drunk I've been."

"Do you have some sort of disease? Cancer? Six months to live?"

James laughed again. "I can't promise I'll still be breathing tomorrow, no more than any lad can, but as far as I know, I'm in the pink."

"Then what is it you don't want to tell me? You think I'll hate you?"

He hesitated.

She gave him a reassuring squeeze. "I love you," she said again.

"Even if I'm not what you think I am?"

"What the hell does that mean?" she snapped. Sudden fear made her voice sharper than she meant it to be, though she didn't know what she was afraid of. Not knowing made it worse. "Have you lied to me?"

"Not once."

"Is your name James Corcoran, or not?"

"Aye, it is."

"Did you, or did you not, promise to protect me?"

"I did."

Are you, or are you not, a member of the New York Police Department?"

He swallowed. "Terry, what you have to understand..."

But she'd already figured it out. She felt suddenly sick to her stomach. Her mind was spinning. "You're not a cop?" she asked in a very small voice.

James took another deep breath. "Terry, I never said I was. Not once. I never showed you a shield, never lied to you."

Teresa snatched her hand back and stared at him as if she was looking at a stranger. In a way, she supposed, she was. "But... but you let me think it. You said..."

"I never lied to you," he repeated. He was gripping the steering wheel very tightly.

She replayed everything she could remember him saying. It was true. He'd never outright told her he wasn't a policeman. But he'd certainly misled her, let her believe what she wanted to believe. He'd never corrected her assumptions. He'd always dodged around the truth.

"But... why?" she asked.

"You'll need to be a bit more specific," he said.

"Why does Detective O'Reilly trust you? You do know her, don't you?"

"She and I go back a good way, as I told you," he said. "I owe her a favor. More than one. And she saved my life."

"Why not send a police officer with me?"

"Erin's of the opinion not everyone in the Department's to be trusted. There's lads on Vinnie the Oil Man's payroll. He's got some of the Feds, too. She needed someone outside organized law enforcement."

"Why didn't she come with me herself?"

James's mouth quirked in a sardonic half-smile. "Don't you understand, Terry? Erin has to stay in New York and pick up the pieces. She needs to spin what happened, so she can get in tight with those bastards in the Lucarellis. She's the one they hired to kill you."

"But... but..." Teresa began. Her mind went into an even tighter spin. "You mean Detective O'Reilly's working for the Mafia?"

"They think she is, aye. But if she was really working for them, and not playacting, we'd not be having this conversation."

"Because I'd be dead."

"Aye."

There was silence in the car for about ninety seconds while Teresa processed the information he'd just given her.

"So how do you fit into all this?" she asked at last.

"I told you. I owed Erin and she cashed in."

"But what do you *do*, if you're not a cop? Are you a soldier? Former military? Private security contractor? Professional bodyguard?"

He shook his head. "I'm none of those things, Terry. I told you once, where I came from, a lad only had a couple of choices. He could be a copper..."

"Or a gangster," she said, remembering. Her mouth went very dry. Suddenly, everything he'd done made sense. The avoidance of the police, the willingness to steal, the skill with hotwiring a car, the roll of cash he carried, the knife... all of it.

James Corcoran, Corky to his friends, was a gangster.

"You're with them," she said in a flat, dead voice.

"I'm with you," he said, finally taking his eyes off the road for a moment. "I told you I'd not let harm come to you, and I meant it. You've naught to fear from me, Terry."

"But you're a member of *la Cosa Nostra*," she said, giving the Italian name for the Mafia.

"Nay. I'm an O'Malley."

"So your name isn't Corcoran?"

"I've told you the truth," he insisted. "I'm James Corcoran, out of Belfast. Evan O'Malley's my employer."

"Who's Evan O'Malley?"

"He's a lad not unlike your friend Vitelli, or Vinnie the Oil Man," James said. "And he thinks Erin works for him."

"I don't understand."

"I don't blame you." James changed lanes to pass a slow-moving Buick. Their car was moving much faster than usual; he was channeling his feelings into his driving. "I suppose it'd be fairer to say, I *worked* for O'Malley. Nowadays I'm something of a free agent. I suppose I should explain a little."

"Please," Teresa said. She was gripping her own elbows. The car's air conditioning was raising goosebumps on her arms. Or maybe it was her nerves giving her the chills.

"My best mate in the world, my whole life long, is a lad name of Carlyle. Morton Carlyle, though no one's called him Morton for a long while. We grew up in Belfast together, on the same street. He's two years older than myself, and a damn sight cleverer. We always looked out for each other. Both of us joined the Brigades when we were teenagers, fought the Brits for a while, but something bad happened to his wife and he shipped out for America. Needed a change of scenery, you ken?"

"What happened to his wife?"

"The UVF murdered her."

"The who?"

"Ulster Volunteer Front. Northern Irish Protestant paramilitary bastards."

"Oh."

"As I was saying, he landed with O'Malley. I'd nothing particular keeping me in Ireland, so I made the voyage to join him. Now, fast-forward a few years and Carlyle fell in with this lass who happens to be a copper. Against his better judgment, he got entangled with her in every possible way. Next thing we all know, she's being asked to do this little job for O'Malley."

"But it's Vitelli who wants me dead," Teresa interrupted.

"Aye, that's so," James agreed. "Things have been a mite dicey between O'Malley and the Lucarellis... that's Vitelli's people. They're no longer at war, but you might say the relationship is... strained. O'Malley agreed to take care of Vitelli's witness problem as a means of reducing tension. And, of course, for money. So Vitelli went to the detective who was running the case, a lass he believes is under Evan's thumb. With Evan's permission, obviously."

"Detective O'Reilly," she said.

"Aye. But as I said, Erin doesn't work for him. Not really. And it's a good thing for you she doesn't. She's been working with Carlyle behind O'Malley's back for a while now, to bring the O'Malleys down from the inside. And you have to understand something, Terry."

"What's that?"

"You can't breathe a word of that to anyone else. Not one soul. I'm putting Erin's life in your hands here. Carlyle's, too. If even a whisper of this comes out before she's ready to move on O'Malley, they're dead. Probably me, too, into the bargain."

Teresa finally understood, or thought she did. "This was a test for her," she said. "Killing me. But why use a car bomb?"

"Carlyle's in possession of a particular set of skills," James said dryly. "You see, he used to build explosives for the Irish Republican Army."

"Oh my."

"I'm no rat, Terry. But I'd never go against my best mate. So since it was a choice between betraying O'Malley and betraying Carlyle, I'd already chosen my side. It's the same one you're on, and a good thing for all of us."

"If it weren't for him, you'd be, what? A professional criminal?"

"Haven't you been listening, love? That's precisely what I am. I don't know how to be anything else."

"God," Teresa said. "So you... you seduced me as part of this undercover plan?"

He winced. "Terry, I'll not deny, as soon as I saw you, it did cross my mind. You're a pretty enough lass, and it's the sort of thing I've done in the past. But that's not what happened."

"It sure looks like it to me."

"Erin ordered me not to. She said she'd cut off a particularly personal part of my anatomy if I so much as laid a hand on you."

"But you slept with me anyway!"

"I didn't know," he said quietly. "This wasn't the plan. You weren't in my plans. You're something outside my experience, Terry. No lass has ever trusted me the way you have, believed in me..."

"But I was believing a lie."

Something crumbled in his face. "I know. And that's why I didn't, why I couldn't tell you. I didn't want to let you down."

Teresa saw his unhappiness, saw the light slipping away from his eyes, and the surge of pity she felt surprised her. Without fully understanding why, she reached out again and laid a hand on his arm. His muscles were so tense that his forearm quivered under her fingertips.

"James," she whispered.

"What?" he replied in a low voice.

"Was it real? What you showed me? What we shared?"

"I thought so, aye."

"So did I. And so maybe..." she broke off.

"Maybe what?"

She didn't finish the thought. He didn't reply.

The remainder of the drive to San Diego was the longest she'd ever seen James Corcoran go without speaking.

*   *   *

From San Diego they went south toward Tijuana and the Mexico border. They got in the southbound lanes for the San Ysidro crossing point. James finally broke his hours-long silence.

"Can you reach into my bag, Terry? There's passports in the outer pocket."

She twisted in her seat and found the requested documents. They looked real and official. She flipped them open and saw she was Elena Lopez, while he went by Andrew Reardon. James's passport was the only one she'd seen which had a smiling photo. Hers appeared to be identical to the one on her driver's license. She wondered how he'd gotten his hands on that picture. Apparently the O'Malley gang had contacts at the DMV.

"Are you really a US citizen?" she asked as she handed his passport over.

He looked surprised. "I'm as American as yourself," he said. "Took the citizenship test and everything."

"Really?"

"Ask me a question about the Constitution."

For the first time since their uncomfortable conversation, she saw a hint of a smile in his eyes. "Okay," she said. "How many amendments are there?"

"Twenty-seven," he said immediately. "But there's really just twenty-five."

"Which ones don't count?"

"Eighteen and twenty-one. The Eighteenth made it illegal to sell alcohol, the dirty gobshites, and the Twenty-First canceled that one out, so they're a wash."

"You know your history," she said.

"I know my liquor," he replied. "We'll be through in no time. For some reason, more lads are trying to get out of Mexico than into it."

"America's never had a big problem keeping people in," Teresa said.

"That's the truth," he agreed. "It's no perfect place, but in my thinking, if you're needing to build walls to keep immigrants out, you must be doing something right. Golden land of opportunity, it is. Did you know there's more Irish-Americans in the world than there are Irish? By a fair margin, too."

It was true, leaving the United States turned out to be a lot easier than getting in. The customs officers gave their passports only a cursory glance. Then they were over the border in Tijuana, driving south.

"Congratulations," James said. "You're now officially an international fugitive."

She gave him a look. "I'm not a fugitive. I'm not wanted by the police."

"If you were, you could do worse. This place is hardly better than Ciudad Juarez. Enjoy the fresh air of freedom, but I'd not advise you to roll down your window until we're out of the city. We're unlikely to be shot at, but you never can tell."

Teresa sighed. "James, is there any place on Earth that's just, well, safe?"

He shrugged. "I grew up in Belfast during the Troubles, remember. You never knew when a lad might toss a petrol bomb your way, or those bastards from the UVF might break down your door and machine-gun you at supper. Safety's something of an illusion wherever you are. It's just that some places make it harder to pretend."

"Did they really do that in Ireland? Machine-gun people at dinner?"

He shrugged again. "They got my best mate's wife that way."

"God. Was he there?"

"Nay. He heard about it after. One of the only times I've ever seen the lad shed tears. His wife was in the family way, too."

"God," she said again. "That's horrible."

"But we're going a little ways down the coast," he said, abruptly changing topics. "To a place I know, name of Playas de Rosarito. It's not the big city. You'll be happier there."

"I was born in the big city."

He smiled. "Then you've no idea what you're missing."

"Is it far?"

"Less than ten miles now. No more than a hop and a jump to a seasoned traveler such as yourself."

*   *   *

Teresa's first glimpse of Mexico was hardly encouraging. James was right; Tijuana was a city which was having more than its fair share of trouble. But she'd seen neighborhoods in New York that were no better, and her sense of perspective had changed a little on this trip. Besides, she told herself, she had a gangster as a tour guide. What could possibly go wrong?

"What's the joke, Terry?" James asked.

She smothered her semi-hysterical giggle. "Nothing."

"You needn't tell me," he said. "I'm only glad you're smiling again."

"Oh, James," she began, but didn't know how to say everything she was thinking.

"It's funny," he said. "You're the only one who calls me that. I'm always Corky or Corks to my friends, as I told you when we first met."

"Do you want me to call you Corky?"

"Nay. It's rather fine being called something special by a particular lass."

"Like a special nickname," she said. "Except in this case, it's your actual name."

"Maybe that makes it even more special," he said.

Their car left the dust of Tijuana in their rearview mirror. The road was uninteresting, the scenery dry brown and dusty green. Teresa settled back in her seat. She was starting to feel like she'd be on the road forever, one motel after another. Without James, she thought, this trip would have been unbearable. With him? It had at least been exciting. But he wasn't who she thought he was. Where did that leave them?

"All right, Terry," James said, pulling off the highway. They passed through an opening in a white cement-block wall and into a small neighborhood. He parked in front of a little white house with a red tile roof. It had a decorative railing around a balcony on the second floor, facing west.

"Is this...?" she began.

"Aye," he said. "It's the end of the journey."

While Teresa was sitting up and unfastening her seatbelt, he was already out of the car, hurrying around to open her door. He bowed slightly, like a coachman escorting a lady to some formal event.

Teresa stood in the street and looked at the house. It was small, by the standards of American homes, but she'd been an apartment-dweller her whole life and it looked like an awful lot of room to her. The walls were bright and clean, fresh-painted. There was practically no yard, but a palm tree grew right next to the front door, a splash of brilliant tropical green.

James had fetched their bags out of the car. "Well?" he asked, coming to stand beside her. "What do you think?"

"I don't know what to think," she said.

"Let's go inside, then," he said. "We'll get you settled." He knelt beside the door and pulled out a loose stone from the walk. Underneath was a key, which he used to unlock the door.

Teresa walked slowly through the house. The ground floor had a small living room, dining room, kitchen, and bathroom, with a fairly new washing machine tucked into an alcove by the back door. Every room was furnished, not expensively but comfortably. She went upstairs and found two bedrooms, another bathroom, and a linen closet. She also discovered the door that led to the balcony. She pulled it open and walked out to the railing.

There, spread out beyond the roof of the next-door house, was the endless blue of the Pacific Ocean. She felt the sea breeze on her face and tasted a hint of salt spray on her lips. It was early evening and the westering sun laid a blazing path across the water, leading straight to her feet.

James was just behind her. He laid a hand on her arm, the first time he'd touched her since his revelation about his past.

"Well?" he asked again.

"It's lovely, James," she sighed, leaning back against him. He felt stiff and tense, but as she nestled closer, he softened.

"That's grand, love," he said, and it struck her that he hadn't called her that all day.

"But who owns this house?" she asked. "And all the furniture and... everything?"

"It's paid for," he said. "You needn't trouble yourself."

"James! You didn't buy a house for me!" She twisted around to look at him, shocked in spite of herself.

He chuckled. "Nay, I didn't," he said. "It's a lease. But the rent's less than you'd think. I called a lad I know, and told him I'd be entertaining a lady. He made all the arrangements. There should be food in the kitchen, cold drinks in the refrigerator. I asked him to lay in a few bottles of tequila."

"First whiskey, now tequila?" she asked, raising an eyebrow.

"Have you never tasted a tequila sunrise?"

She shook her head.

"I'll make you one," he said. "Stay right where you are. I'll not be a moment."

Teresa was in no hurry. She felt she could stay where she was, looking out at the ocean, for hours. The light was almost painfully bright, but she didn't care. The limitless expanse of the ocean, on the opposite side of the continent from New York, intoxicated her with its sense of wide-open freedom. In spite of what James had said, she did feel safe. She felt almost like she'd come home.

The door opened again behind her. James stepped in close and put a glass in her hand. It was a beautiful drink, orange blending into crimson, topped with an orange slice and a cherry garnish. He'd made one for himself, too. He clinked glasses with her.

"It's more of a morning beverage, of course," he said. "But perhaps it's appropriate, to mark your new beginning."

She nodded and took a sip. She tasted the sweetness of the grenadine, twining together on her tongue with the tart orange juice. It was a bright, refreshing, wholesome taste, with a hint of wild intoxication under the surface.

"James?" she asked quietly.

"Aye?"

"Are you staying?"

"Aye," he said again. "You need to get settled, and I need to make certain you're squared away proper."

"That wasn't what I meant," she said. "I meant, will you stay... here?"

"Of course. There's the spare bedroom. I'll be close if you're needing anything."

Teresa felt frustrated and embarrassed. Could he possibly not know what she was trying to say? "No. James, that's not... I mean, what I'm saying is, do you want... can you... will you stay? With me?"

He looked surprised. "You want me to?"

There was a lump in her throat. She nodded. "I don't want you to go."

"Even with me being... what I am?"

"You're James Corcoran," she said. She gathered her courage, reached up, and touched his cheek. He flinched at the contact, but she didn't draw back. She traced the line of his cheek, careful not to brush against the bandage where Lou's hook had gashed him. "James, why won't you let anybody love you?"

He looked away. "I've never known anyone who'd want to."

"Nonsense," she said, her schoolteacher voice surfacing for a moment. "Everybody's lovable, James, and you more than most."

"I tricked you into it," he said, looking back at her. "I fooled you."

"You showed me the real you," she said, keeping her hand on his face, holding the contact between them. "It was my choice, loving you, every step of the way. I'm sorry for whatever happened to you, all the things that made you think you're a bad man, but you're not! You're a good man, you've been good to me, and you're *my* good man! So you're going to let me love you, James, if it's the last thing either of us does! I'm not asking anymore, I'm telling you. You're staying right here, with me!"

"Aren't you scared of me?"

"No. I was, for a little while, but then I remembered."

"What was it you remembered?"

"Everything." Her own smile was wistful. "Your kindness, the way you make me laugh, the way you make me feel safe. I've been scared too much, James. I can't be scared of you. You're my lifeline. If you really were a bad man, you would've hurt me."

"I still could. Terry, I should go. Before—"

"No! I told you, you're staying!"

A smile started in his eyes, twinkling there like the sunlight on the ocean, and spread to his cheeks, then his mouth. "Giving orders now, love?"

"Just the one," she said, feeling an answering smile fighting to break through the firm determination she'd put in her jaw.

"Yes, ma'am," he said. "But you're certain you're only giving the one order? You've got me here, in a particularly chastened and obedient frame of mind. Haven't you any further instructions?"

"Well," she said, taking a half step closer and letting her hand trail down his cheek to the side of his neck. "You could kiss me."

"I could, at that," he said. Then he bent down and kissed her, there on the balcony overlooking the Pacific, and to Teresa it was like none of the fear or anger or confusion mattered anymore. There was just the sweetness of that moment, of knowing it had all been worth it, and she felt tears in her eyes, but they were tears of pure joy.

*   *   *

"James?" Teresa said quietly.

He made a muffled, sleepy sound.

She turned her head to look at him, being careful not to move too quickly. His arm was around her, his body warm against her back. She saw him as a shadowy silhouette. The sun had gone down, and they hadn't taken the time to turn on the lights. They'd been thinking about other things. Her new bed, she had to admit, was very comfortable.

"James?" she said again.

"What's the matter, love?" he murmured.

"I need to ask you something. Now that we've done... what we did."

"Fire ahead."

"I need you awake."

"I'm awake."

"Stay."

"Beg pardon?" He still sounded sleepy, but a little more alert.

"Stay."

"I'll be here in the morning, no fear."

"I don't mean here, in my bed. And I don't mean just for tonight."

He raised himself on one elbow. She tried to read his expression in the dark. It was hard to see what was in his eyes.

"Terry, I've told you, I'll make sure you're safe and well settled."

"James," she said, "you're not listening. Don't go back to New York."

"Terry, my whole life's there. My work, my friends... everything." He paused. "Everything except you."

She felt suddenly wretched. "I know," she said, speaking quickly, almost babbling as she tried to get everything out. "I don't have any right. I've only known you a few days. And it's crazy, this whole thing. I know it's your job to take care of me. Well, not your job, I guess, not really, but the only thing you promised was you'd get me here. And you did it, and I'm grateful. For protecting me and... and for everything else. But New York is no good for you. If you go back, you'll slide back into your old life. You'll be just a gangster again, and you'll go back to hating yourself, and you'll leave me behind. And I don't want to ask, but..."

"Hush, love," he said, putting a finger against her lips. He brought his face close to hers and kissed her, moving his hand to cup her cheek affectionately. "It's all right. I told you, Terry. We've had a grand time here, but I'm not the lad for you to fall for. I don't want to break your heart. I've warned you more than once."

"But don't you see, James? It's too late. You can't help it anymore. If you leave, you'll break it. And you said you'd stay!"

"You said it, Terry," he said quietly. "Not me."

"But you said yes! You promised!"

"How long will you want me?" he asked, and he pulled away from her, sitting up in bed. "I know, right now it's grand, everything's magical, but that magic doesn't last. Someday you'll wake up and you'll look at me and what you'll see isn't what you've dreamed of. It'll just be Corky Corcoran, that flash bastard from Belfast with his slick smile and his way with the ladies, and you'll want to be rid of him."

"James!" she said sharply. "Don't say that!"

"It's the truth."

"You don't know that! Stop it!"

"What?"

"If you want to leave, say so, but don't you dare put it on me! Don't you dare try to make it my fault!"

He was startled, she could tell. "That's not what I meant."

"Yes it is! I told you, you have to let me love you. That's not up to you!"

"Are you angry with me?"

"Yes!" Teresa sat up, grabbed her pillow, and swung it. James was fast, but she caught him completely off guard. The pillow smacked into the side of his head and knocked him sprawling. He lay there, rubbing his head in stunned shock.

"Oh, God," she exclaimed. "I'm sorry! I forgot about your head! Your stitches! I didn't mean to—"

James started laughing. Lying on his back, one hand at his face, his shoulders shook with mirth.

Teresa stared at him. In the dim light, she still couldn't tell what he was feeling, whether he was angry or amused or insane. "James," she began.

"A Mafia button man couldn't do for me," he said, still laughing. "But a schoolteacher from Brooklyn, she blindsided me. Me, Corky Corcoran, whacked by a bloody pillow! I hope the lads back in New York never get wind of it. I'd never hear the end of it!"

Teresa peered more closely at him. "Are you all right?" she asked.

James's hands moved so fast, she didn't even see them. He snatched up the sheets from his waist and whipped them around her, bundling her tight and wrestling her down onto the mattress. Teresa gave a startled squawk and struggled. It was like trying to wrangle a sea otter. James twisted free and rolled on top of her. He bent in and planted a kiss squarely on her lips.

Teresa put out a hand blindly, finding his pillow and bringing it in from the side, hitting him a glancing blow. James snatched up the other pillow. The two of them pummeled each other, like two kids at a sleepover. Now she was laughing too, at the sheer absurdity of it all.

He caught her wrist mid-swing with one hand. She grabbed his other arm with her hand. For a second they were face to face, breathing hard, caught mid-laugh. Then they locked their lips together, moving in answer to a simultaneous impulse, and fell back onto the bed, kicking the sheets out of the way.

"All right, love, you win," James gasped, a few minutes later. She was lying on top of him, their chests rising and falling in time with their breathing. Their bodies were slippery with sweat, the bedclothes strewn all over the floor.

"I do?"

"Aye," he said. "I'll stay."

"You're not just saying that?"

"Word of honor."

"And not just because of this?" She moved her hips against him.

"Because of you, Terry," he said, answering her movement with one of his own that made her suck in her breath and bite her lower lip.

"I love you, James."

"All right," he said again.

"All right?" she repeated, raising herself so she could look in his face. "That's all?"

"I believe you."

She knew that was a hard thing for him to say, but she couldn't just leave it at that. "And...?"

"And what?"

"Do you?"

"Do I?"

She moved against him again, teasingly, demandingly. "Do you love me?"

"Terry," he said, "I'm no good at this."

"I beg to differ."

"I don't really know what to do with a girl, once I've got her in bed and we've done what we came for. I'm good at that part."

"Yes," she said. "You certainly are."

"But I've no idea where we go from here."

"Neither do I," she said. "It'll be an adventure."

"Aye," he said. "It will, at that."

"But you'll stay."

"Until when?"

"Until I tell you to go."

He thought it over. "Fair enough. I promise, I'll stay as long as you'll have me."

"It won't be so bad," she said. "I promise."

"Enjoying this position of power, are you?"

She bent down and kissed him, lightly nipping at his mouth. She dug her fingertips into his chest and felt him squirm. "Yes," she whispered. "Isn't it obvious?"

"You've a bit of wildcat in you, Terry," he said. "I'd no idea."

"Neither did I. You're the one who woke her up and let her out. So really, this is your fault."

"I'm not the least bit sorry."

*   *   *

The airplane rolled to a stop at the gate. Teresa and Norma unbuckled their seatbelts and stood, stretching their stiff legs.

"You're a sweet girl, Elena," Norma said. "Your young man is lucky to have you. It must have been hard, being all the way across the country."

"Separation from the people you love is painful," Teresa said.

"I wish you'd tell me the rest of your story," Norma said. "I can see you thinking about it, remembering it. You keep giving me these little hints and suggestions."

"I'm sorry," Teresa said. "I don't mean to be rude. It's just... I don't trust people easily."

"Of course, dear," Norma said. "But will you still let my son give you a ride to the hospital?"

That much, surely, could do no harm. In fact, it might help. A family of strangers was perfect camouflage.

"I shouldn't have let him go," Teresa said as they wrestled their carry-on bags down from the overhead compartments and waited for the crowd of passengers in the aisle to thin out.

"Why did you? Was it for work? Or did you have a fight?"

"Nothing like that," she said. "Maybe it's just that we can't get away from what we've done. Not completely. There was... unfinished business."

"Something in your past, dear? Or his?"

"Both."

Chapter 12

Teresa lived in a happy dream of sun, sand, and sea. She and James walked on the beach, swam in the ocean, and sat on the balcony of her house, soaking up the sun. Its rays felt warmer than she remembered in Brooklyn, even on fine summer days. The Pacific was the most beautiful blue she'd ever seen.

"Being dead isn't so bad now, is it, Terry?" James asked her. He called her that when they were alone. In public, she was always Elena.

"No, it's not," she agreed. "Dying's the hard part. Once you're dead, you're fine."

He laughed and kissed her.

Gradually, as the days went by, they explored the town. Playas de Rosarito had its tourist traps and hotels, further up the beach, but they avoided those. Teresa preferred to spend time getting to know the locals, trying to wrap her head around the language. She knew a little Spanish from her teaching days, and quickly picked up more. She met a few of the nearby families, all of whom seemed friendly. She was worried at first about what she'd say once they asked about her history, but no one pried into her prior life.

"Do you wonder about that, love?" James asked when she mentioned it to him. "You're down here with a lad who's obviously in the Life."

"What do you mean?"

He smiled. "I've the tattoos and scars. I pay cash for everything. And I'm a *gringo*. I'm a right scoundrel, to anyone who knows what to look for."

"I thought you were a cop," she said, pouting a little.

"These people see drug dealers and killers on their streets," he reminded her. "The only *gringos* who come down here are tourists and gangsters. And I fear I'm not acting the part of a tourist."

"But what about me?"

"Clearly, you're my girl," he said, putting a hand against her cheek. "That's good enough for them. We're causing no trouble, hurting no one, so they're asking no questions. I may be a gangster, but I'm a well-behaved one. If we're running from something, it's none of their concern."

"James," she said. "If I'm not a tourist, what am I? I like the vacation, don't get me wrong. But shouldn't I be doing something? Eventually I'll go crazy, just sitting around."

"What do you want to do?"

She shrugged. "I don't know. I've always been a teacher."

"Did you like it?"

"Yes. I love kids."

"Why not do it here?"

"What? You mean teach in a Mexican school?"

"Why not?" he repeated.

"I hardly speak Spanish, for starters."

"You speak English."

"Most of these kids don't."

"My point exactly."

"You think they need an English teacher?"

"That's a grand idea, Terry."

"No it isn't. They'll check my credentials."

He was already laughing quietly, shaking his head. "Terry, you really don't understand, do you? Sure, if you're wanting to teach at some private academy, they might look close at your bona fides. But anywhere else? If you've a certification to teach and a work visa, you're set."

"I don't have either of those," she said.

"Yet," he said, winking.

"James! You can't get me a fake teaching certificate!"

"Of course I can. Easiest thing in the world, love. I know a lad. I'll make a couple of calls. Inside a week, two at the most, you'll be a certified English teacher."

"That's... that's... teaching fraud!"

"Hmm," James said, pretending to be impressed. "That does sound serious. And I admit, it's one crime I never thought to commit. I've no idea what the penalties are. I suppose, since I've only faked up an official United States passport for you, under an assumed name, I don't want to fudge you a certificate for something you're actually qualified to do. That'd be downright wrong."

"James! Be serious!"

"I am serious, love." He took both her hands in his. "If this is what you're wanting to be doing, we'll make it happen. Do you think you wouldn't be able to teach them?"

"Well... no..."

"Are you afraid for the bairns you'll be teaching? You think you'll be a bad influence on them?"

"No!"

"The parents, then?"

"They know I'm a gangster's girlfriend, according to you."

"Every one of these people knows someone in the Life, I guarantee it. Most of them have family who've done something or other. It's a part of their daily existence."

"Well..." Teresa felt herself weakening. "I would like to be in a classroom again."

He smiled broadly. "Grand! That's settled, then! I'll find you an opening and get you an interview as soon as we've cleared up the paperwork."

* * *

That was how Elena Lopez ended up with an official certification to teach English in Mexico. James worked his behind-the-scenes magic on the authorities, and inside a week Teresa had an interview with the superintendent of the elementary school. He was delighted with her qualifications, only some of which were faked, and before she knew it, she had a job teaching English to third-graders.

The school year was already in swing, but that was the sort of technicality James was an expert at rendering irrelevant. Soon enough, Teresa found herself buying schoolbooks, along with an assortment of conservative blouses and skirts to ensure she made a good impression on the parents.

She was nervous, standing outside the elementary school, until she reminded herself it wasn't that long since a Mafia assassin had tried to murder her in a motel bathroom. Handling a bunch of nine-year-old Mexican boys and girls couldn't be that bad.

She loved it. Teresa had always liked pre-teen kids. They were that wonderful age where they wanted to learn everything, before adolescent hormones addled their brains. Her Spanish was good enough to get by and they all wanted to learn English. When she asked, on the first day of class, how many of them had been to the United States, not one child raised a hand. Then she asked how many wanted to go, and every single hand in the room shot up. Many had relatives who'd crossed the border. They couldn't get enough stories about the United States. Teresa wasn't used to being exotic and fascinating. It was a new and pleasant experience.

"I should read fairy tales to the kids," she said one evening over dinner.

"Aye?" James said. "Are they good for learning English?"

"Yes," she said. "But mainly because I'm living in one."

He laughed. "And this is the part where you live happily ever after, is it?"

She laid a hand on his on the tabletop. "Maybe."

James was working too. He didn't share many details, but she understood he was using his shipping contacts and expertise. Teresa suspected him of smuggling. He was definitely bringing in money from somewhere, and he kept unusual hours, often coming in very late at night. But he always had a smile and a kiss for her, and he never came back with blood on his clothes or any sign of injuries, so she didn't ask questions and she tried not to worry.

Days turned into weeks. Teresa's days were filled with her job, sun, sea, and warmth. And at night she had James. No matter how late he came in, he never failed to show her how glad he was to see her. The warmth in his bright green eyes, the touch of his fingertips, the way he could make her feel like the most beautiful woman on Earth, everything about him really did make her feel like she was living a fairy tale romance.

"James?" she finally asked, late one night. They were lying in bed, both of them naked. He had come home early on this particular evening, surprising her in the living room. He'd slipped his hands around her waist and nuzzled into her neck, kissing her on the side of her throat in a way that always made her knees go weak. They had made love on the couch, quickly and passionately, and then again upstairs, more slowly and tenderly. Now she lay on her belly, feeling the warm afterglow in her skin and watching the orange and pink of the sunset through the west windows.

"Aye?" He lazily traced a fingertip down her backbone.

"Are you happy here?"

"Can you ask that? Isn't it obvious?"

"Do you miss New York?"

He sighed. "I suppose I do. But then, I miss Ireland every so often, too, and I'm not likely to be living there again. It's possible to be happy where you are, while still feeling a bit of a pang for the places and people you've left behind."

"I guess I'll have to go back there, for the trial, at least," she said.

"Aye."

"But I can't stay there. They'll come after me. The Lucarellis, I mean. After Mr. Vitelli goes to jail."

"They may not bother," James said. "Damage done and all that. The Mafia's not what it used to be, love. But you've a point. It's a danger, however slight."

"Can we come back here? After?"

"Love, you can go anywhere in the wide world."

"I didn't mean just me."

He kept stroking her back, leaving delicious tingling trails of sensation on her sensitive skin. Teresa purred. That was the only word she could think of that fit. She arched against him, feeling very feline.

"You know," he said, "you're the only lass who's stuck with me this long."

"I can't believe that," she said, turning her head to look at him. "Isn't it you who's left them, not the other way round?"

"Well..." he said, his eyes sliding to the side. "I'd not want anyone to be saddled with me."

"James, do you really think I'm doing you a favor here?"

He laughed. "I'd like to think you're getting something out of it, true."

"I think you get scared they'll really get to know you," she said. "And then they'll leave you. So you leave first. That way you don't have to worry about it."

"You're a primary-school teacher, Terry, not a shrink. Are you really qualified to be analyzing me?"

She rose up on her elbows and looked him over. "Let's see. I know your mother made a point of telling you what a disappointment you were to her, how you reminded her of your dad. I know he was kind of a loser. You're good with girls, but you don't let them in if you can help it. I'd guess you didn't get much affection at home, so you went looking for it outside the house. You probably found someone when you were pretty young, I'd say—"

She broke off suddenly. There was a look in James's eyes she'd never seen there before. She saw something open, raw, and bleeding in his soul, and the naked pain in his look horrified her. It was only there for a moment, then he covered it up again, but she knew she hadn't imagined it. That was a look that could haunt her dreams.

"And so I fill the empty place in my life with all the things that make me feel good," he said in a quiet, easy tone. "Strong drink and sex, mostly. That's hardly a secret, love."

"James? What happened to you? When you were a boy?"

"A great many things," he said. "If you're wanting stories, I can give you a few. There was one time, my mate Carlyle and I—"

She put out her hand and touched his face. "James," she said again, gently. "What happened to you?"

The smile dropped off his face again. "Terry, this isn't exactly proper pillow talk."

"You can tell me," she said. "I want to know."

"Nay, lass. You don't."

"I'm not afraid. You can trust me."

"I don't want your pity, Terry."

"Why not?" she asked. "I love you. You know that. Whatever you tell me won't change that. God! If I can handle you being a gangster, I can take whatever this is."

He swallowed. He actually looked nervous. Teresa watched him closely, making sure to keep her own expression open and accepting. She'd had training at her old school in how to spot the red flags in a child, indicators of abuse or neglect, and James, despite his age, was showing more than one of them.

"You're right about my mum and da," he said, and he looked away. "Do you know, I can't remember my mum ever giving me a kiss or a hug? Not once."

Teresa felt a crack run through her heart at those words. She wanted to throw her arms around him, hold on just as tight as she could, but she didn't dare interrupt, now that he'd started talking.

"I was lucky," he went on, speaking in a flat monotone now. "There was a lad in the neighborhood, my parish priest, who took an interest in me. He saw I was lonely, and he took to talking with me after school. I was an altar boy, you'll remember. He spent a lot of time getting to know me, made me feel at home in the church. He recognized what I was missing, and he made sure I knew how special I was."

A little worm of nausea writhed in Teresa's stomach. She knew what James was talking about. She tried to think what to say. While she was deciding, he kept talking without inflection, very much unlike his usual, animated voice.

"He told me God loved me, and so did he. He used to... pray with me. At least, that's what he called it."

"How old were you?" Teresa whispered.

"Nine, or thereabouts. It went on until I was twelve. After that, I suppose I got too old for him."

It was Teresa's turn to swallow. She put a hand out, she couldn't help herself, and laid it on his shoulder. She felt the muscles in his neck, so tense they were standing out against his skin.

"That was when I started getting interested in the colleens, you ken? The lasses? A bit early, I know, but what can a lad do? Besides, it couldn't be too sinful if it was the sort of thing a priest did, could it?"

"Oh, James," Teresa said through her tears.

The spell broke. He looked at her with the usual warmth back in his eyes. His familiar, easy smile spread over his face again. "Terry, love, don't you go looking at me like that. It's ancient history, and it's nothing to do with you or me."

"James," she said quietly, "you said you wouldn't lie to me."

"I've told you the truth," he said sharply.

"I don't mean about your past," she said. "I mean, it's not just in your past. It's a part of you, here and now. But it wasn't your fault."

"I don't follow your thread, love."

"You were just a boy," she said. "A little boy who was desperate to feel loved. That man took advantage of you. It wasn't your fault."

He shrugged. "Maybe not. There's precious little I can do about it now. I suppose it's fortunate Carlyle never found out about it."

"Why not?"

"He'd have blown up the church, I imagine, and if that's not a one-way ticket to Hell, I don't know what is. Even then, that lad was good with a bomb."

James smiled as he said it, but Teresa was quite sure he wasn't joking. She remembered how the car outside the hotel had exploded and knew Carlyle was quite capable of blowing up a church if he wanted to.

"James?"

"Aye?"

"Thank you for telling me."

"This is nothing a lass really wants to hear."

"James," she said, "look at me."

He did. Whatever else he was, James Corcoran was no coward.

"I love you," she said.

"That's right fine of you to say," he said.

"James," she said again, "I love you."

He looked perplexed. "Aye, you just said that."

"And I'm going to keep saying it, until you believe me. I love you. All of you. Maybe your mom didn't love you. She should have, but that's her fault, not yours. And I'm not her. And that... that man didn't love you, not the way you need to be loved. I love you, James Corcoran."

She took him in her arms and held him. They were naked, but it wasn't a sensual embrace. He was stiff and tense in her arms, and then he softened. His arms went around her in return, clutching her to him. She felt a muffled, choking sound in his chest and realized it was a suppressed sob. If she'd been able to talk to one of his O'Malley associates, they might have told her no one had ever seen Corky Corcoran cry. It wouldn't have surprised her to hear that. But here and now, he was crying in her arms, and she held him until his tears ran dry and he fell asleep. Teresa lay beside him, and after a while, his quiet breathing lulled her to sleep as well.

*   *   *

The bustle at JFK Airport made Teresa's head swim. San Diego was a big city, too, but this was New York. This was home. And it didn't feel like home anymore. Her old life, the apartment in Brooklyn, the classroom, all of it seemed enormously distant and long ago. As Norma led the way through the baggage claim, chattering cheerfully the whole time, Teresa felt like she was aimlessly drifting, as if she were some sort of ghost.

Maybe she was dead. Maybe the real Teresa Tommasino had died in a car bomb, and what was left was a wandering spirit. She'd gone far away, on a sort of spectral vacation, and now she was coming back, like a woman in some old horror story by Edgar Allan Poe.

"Are you all right, dear?" Norma asked.

"What?" Teresa said, startled out of her thoughts. "Oh. Yes. Of course."

"It'll be all right," Norma said. "My son should be outside waiting for us. We'll get you to the hospital straightaway, don't worry."

The old woman was right. They hadn't been standing at the curb more than a minute when a big Oldsmobile worked its way over to them and honked a greeting. A young man who looked to be in his early twenties popped the trunk and hopped out of the car, running around the fender.

"Hey, Nana!" he said, giving her a quick hug. "How was the flight?"

"Wonderful, dear," Norma said. She turned to Teresa. "Elena, this is my grandson. Mark, this is Elena Lopez. I sat next to her on the plane. She's here to visit her boyfriend. He's in the hospital. I told her we'd be happy to give her a ride."

"Uh, sure," Mark said, surprised. He offered his hand. "Good to meet you, Ms. Lopez. Mark Stanford. Did Grandma happen to find out which hospital your friend is in?"

"Bellevue," Teresa said.

"Oh, good." He smiled. "That's on our way, more or less. Do you have any luggage?"

"Only this," Teresa said, hefting her little suitcase.

"Okay. You can put it in the trunk. Welcome to New York! Have you been here before?"

"Yes," she said. "But not for a long time."

Chapter 13

Neither of them talked about what had happened the previous night. James didn't seem any different to Teresa when she headed off to school. He made tequila sunrises to go with their toast and omelets, which still seemed awfully decadent. She wondered what her mom would think of a woman who drank tequila for breakfast. But when he kissed her goodbye, he held on to her hands a little longer, and she thought she saw a softness in his eyes that hadn't been there before.

But maybe she'd imagined it, because when she got home after school, he was waiting with a gift for her. It was a small box, too big for jewelry but too small for anything else she could think of. It was black molded plastic and looked somehow ominous.

"James?" she asked, looking at it but not taking it. "What is this?"

"Something for my peace of mind," he said. "I'll admit, I'm not completely comfortable about this, but I'll feel better if you've got it, if you're ever all alone here at night."

He opened the box to reveal a black, snub-nosed revolver.

Teresa just stared at it, making no move to touch it. She'd have been happier with a live rattlesnake.

"Go on," he said. "Pick it up. It's unloaded, though you'd do well to check that for yourself. Never take another lad's word when it comes to firearms."

Very carefully, she picked up the pistol. It felt surprisingly heavy in her hand. She made certain it was aimed at the floor.

"What am I supposed to do with this?" she asked.

"Nothing, I hope. But it's better to have it and not need it."

"Where did you get it?"

"I know a lad. Here, I'll show you the workings." He came to stand beside her and quickly, deftly demonstrated how to open the cylinder and work the mechanism. "Slide the rounds in from the back here, then snap the cylinder in place. You can cock the hammer if you want, it'll make your first trigger pull easier, but you needn't if there's no time. The grand thing about a revolver is you can keep it loaded without wearing anything out. An automatic puts strain on the springs in the magazine, and if it sits too long, it'll jam on you. This won't. I'm thinking you'd best keep it in the drawer at your side of the bed, close to hand and fully loaded."

"James? Why are you giving me this now?"

He smiled reassuringly. "I've some business up north, at the border. I'll be gone two nights, maybe three. But you needn't fret. Nothing's going to happen. I'll just feel better knowing you've got it, just in case. Now, hold it like this." He moved behind her and guided her hands up, helping her take aim.

"Now listen to me, love," he said. "This is important. Only aim at something, or someone, you're prepared to shoot. Don't ever point a gun at a man just to threaten him. Only take it out if you're willing to use it. Otherwise, you'd best be running and screaming for help. And most of the time, that's a better bet for you. But if you need to shoot, sight down the barrel and let him get to about ten feet from you, no closer but not much further, either."

"Why so close?"

"It's no easy thing, shooting a lad," James said quietly. "Your hands won't be as steady as you'd wish. Father out and you'll miss, like as not. And don't try anything fancy. Don't aim for the head, or think to shoot him in the leg. Aim dead center and squeeze the trigger. Don't jerk your hand back, just squeeze, smooth and strong. The revolver will jump in your hand, so keep your wrists firm. It'll make the devil's own racket and startle the both of you. But you'll be expecting it and he won't. As soon as you can, bring the barrel back on target and give him two more shots, no matter if you hit him the first time or not. If you hit him with the first one, he'll make an easier target, that's all. Never count on just one bullet. If a lad's worth shooting, he's worth shooting more than once. Assuming he goes down, give him another, just to be sure. That'll leave you two rounds for emergencies."

"Emergencies?" she echoed, incredulous.

"Like if he brought a friend." James had been very serious. Now he smiled. "Nothing's going to happen, love. I'm hoping you'll put this toy away and never have reason to pull it out again. But for now, let's practice dry-firing a few times. I'd suggest using live ammunition, but the neighbors might take issue."

Because he wanted her to, not because she thought it would be useful, Teresa did as he asked. She practiced pulling the pistol's trigger while fending off imaginary attackers. Then, under James's watchful eye, she loaded the gun and put it in the nightstand, shuddering a little as she did. Maybe he felt safer with her in possession of a gun, but she didn't.

*   *   *

James left after supper, with a lingering kiss and an affectionate smile. He drove north toward Tijuana. Teresa watched the car disappear into the twilight and told herself not to worry. He was more than a match for anything that might come after him.

She busied herself with schoolwork, housecleaning, shopping; all the normal, everyday business of living. But her life felt hollow and strange. She'd just been getting used to living in Mexico with James, and now here she was, all on her own.

What if he didn't come back?

The moment she had that thought, she wished she could rewind time to before she'd thought it. Once it was in her head, there was no getting rid of it. He was doing something illegal, associating with people who could provide him with things like the gun in their bedroom. He was a mobster, a career criminal. The Mob killed people. They did it all the time. They'd tried to kill her and very nearly succeeded.

She told herself James was fast, smart, and lucky. But that was no consolation. She knew just how close Fishhook Lou had come to killing both of them.

Even if something hadn't happened to him, what if he'd just... left? What if he had no intention of hanging around? He'd gotten what he wanted from her. He'd done what he'd agreed to do. He'd gotten her safely out of the country, under a false name. She was safe. What if he'd gone back to New York, to his old life, leaving her with nothing but memories?

"No," she said out loud. "No, he told me he'd stay. He promised."

How many abandoned women had said that cheap, pitiful phrase over the years? How many had said it about James Corcoran?

Teresa told herself she was different. She was special. He'd let her in. He'd showed her his real self, the hurt little boy hiding inside the brash, confident man. She loved him, and she believed he loved her.

But her heart wouldn't listen to her logic. The first night was bad. She hardly slept, starting awake at every sound. The night hid a thousand invisible, imagined assassins. The darkness promised nothing but loneliness, now and forever.

After two endless hours lying awake in bed, tossing and turning, she got up and worked on a vocabulary quiz for her students. Then she started the coffee pot and waited for sunrise.

Fortified by lots and lots of coffee, she got through that day. Her attention wandered, both from fatigue and from worry. When one of the kids, a rambunctious boy named Miguel, managed to tip his desk over, spilling pencils and paper across the floor, she snapped at him so sharply that the little boy burst into tears. She was immediately contrite, comforting him, but the damage was done. The kid shied away from her for the rest of the day.

The second night was a little better, mainly because she was completely exhausted. She didn't so much sleep as lose consciousness, falling into a black hole of forgetfulness. When she woke up, she still felt bad, but at least she was better rested.

She managed to forget herself for a while in her work, finding that the busier she kept, the less she thought. She tried to throw herself into her lessons, concentrating on verbs and nouns. But missing James was like a physical ache in her belly.

Why hadn't they installed a phone? Maybe it was a security thing. He wouldn't want her calling him in the middle of something sensitive. As far as she knew, he hadn't even brought a cell phone from New York. The whole point was to disappear, after all, and cell phones could be traced. But why, oh why hadn't he thought to set up a phone so he call her and let her know he was okay?

She hurried home right after school. James wasn't back yet. He'd said two nights, maybe three. She cleaned the house, though it was already spotless. She cooked a nice dinner. She was trying a recipe for empanadas she'd gotten from the mom of one of her kids. A woman named Elena Lopez, she'd realized, might come across as a little odd if all she knew how to cook was pasta and peppers. She was trying hard to learn the local cuisine.

Dinner was ready just before six. No sign of James. She held off on eating, hoping against hope that he would be home for a late dinner. The thought of cooking a fine, big meal and then eating it alone was too sad and pitiful to contemplate.

In the end, she ate a cold empanada a little before eight and put the rest in the fridge. She took a shot of tequila, then another.

It didn't mean anything. He'd said it might be three nights.

She wished they'd gotten a television. It would've made her feel less alone.

Teresa went to bed close to midnight. It was amazing how empty it felt, sleeping alone. She'd done it her whole life, but now she wanted James.

* * *

Headlights shone through the window. A car's engine rumbled outside and died away into silence. Teresa climbed out of bed. She hurried down the stairs, trailing one hand on the wall, and ran on bare feet to the front door. She yanked the door open and stepped out onto the walk. James's car stood in front of the house. She saw his familiar silhouette behind the wheel.

The headlights switched off. She raise a hand in greeting, relief blossoming in her.

The car exploded.

The fireball spiraled up into the sky. The car windows shattered outward, spinning scimitars of glass slashing the air all around her. By some dark miracle, none of them struck her. She heard a wicked whistle as a bit of glass passed her ear close enough to twitch her hair aside. The car was an inferno. The heat on her face was like the mouth of a furnace.

Teresa flung her hands to her mouth as if she could hold in the terrible wail that came up from the pit of her stomach.

She woke gasping, drenched in sweat. Her heart was pounding. For a moment all she could do was lie there, panting for breath. It had been so real.

Had the nightmare woken her, or had she heard something? Maybe her subconscious had noticed a car outside. Maybe James was back. She listened.

She heard a faint, soft tinkling sound downstairs. It reminded her of the sound a drinking glass made when dropped. Broken glass on tile.

Teresa tried to listen harder, over the beat of her own pulse in her ears. There was a soft click. It sounded like the bolt on the front door.

Fear rose up around her, as if the night was trying to smother her. She didn't hear anything else, and somehow that was worse. Someone was in the house, downstairs. For a wild moment she wondered if it was James. Might he have forgotten his key? He could have broken a window to let himself in.

Teresa knew better.

Her tongue felt thick and swollen in her mouth. She tried to swallow, but her throat was too dry. She thought of the back door. Maybe, if she ran, she could make it. No. Too far. The intruder was already inside, in the living room. He could already be on the stairs.

Moving slowly, trying not to make a sound, she reached for the nightstand. She very carefully eased open the drawer and felt inside. Her fingertips brushed the oiled steel of the revolver.

"Don't ever point a gun at a man just to threaten him," James had said. Could she do it? Shoot someone?

Teresa didn't know. Did she dare?

Maybe it was a burglar. Maybe he'd just look around the downstairs, take what he could carry, and leave. She didn't have much that would interest a thief. In America, you could turn on a light and shout and most burglars would run away. What would happen here? She couldn't call the police; she had no phone.

There was a soft scuffing sound on the stairs, on the landing. The man was coming up. Toward her.

Teresa slid out of bed. The floorboards were cool under her bare feet. She was wearing only a long T-shirt and underwear. Her legs were bare. She felt very vulnerable. Had she loaded the gun? She couldn't remember. Her thoughts were wild things, scrambling around her head like trapped mice.

She turned to face the bedroom door, bringing up the pistol, trying to remember everything James had told her. She remembered now, it was loaded. She'd watched him slide the bullets into the cylinder. She was sure of it. Holding the gun in both hands, she brought it up to point at the door. The barrel wavered. Her hands were shaking, just like he'd warned her they would.

A footstep, quiet but distinct, sounded just outside the bedroom door. Teresa held her breath. Surely he must hear her heart. It was pounding so loudly it might wake the next-door neighbors, like the dead man's heart in that old story by Poe.

The doorknob began to turn.

The door swung silently open. A man stood in the doorway, half-hidden in shadows. He stepped into the room. Moonlight slanting through the blinds reflected on a shining crescent in his right hand.

It was another nightmare. It had to be.

Fishhook Lou Andreotti paused. He saw her standing there. Even in the dark, he must have seen the gun in her hands. But if he had, it didn't seem to bother him.

"Hey, babe," he said, giving her a smile that in other circumstances might have been friendly. "Long time no see. I know, this is a little unexpected. Sorry to barge in like this." He took a step toward her.

"Don't." Her voice was high-pitched, almost a squeak.

"Hey, look," he said, spreading his hands in an absurdly nonthreatening gesture. The moonlight glinted on the cargo hook in his right hand. "I'm not here for you. You know that. I didn't hurt you last time, babe. It'd be a shame to mark up that pretty bod of yours." He gave her legs an appreciative glance and took another step toward her.

"Stop," she said, trying to steady her voice and her hands. "I'll do it." He was nine or ten feet away. Ten feet, no closer, James had said. She tried to pull the trigger. Her finger refused to move. She felt hypnotized.

"It's okay," he said, holding out his left hand. "I get it. I scared you. And you're scared now. But you can just hand that to me, and I'll take care of everything. It's cool, babe." He took another step.

"How?" she whispered, unable to complete the question.

"Oh, your boy, Corky, he's been hanging around the wrong people," Lou said. "Coyotes know people, and I know some of the same people. You know what a coyote is? That's one of those boys who runs illegals across the border. Corky's a smuggler, you know, and he's real good at it. But it's a small community, if you know what I'm saying. I heard a redheaded white boy had started running wetbacks and I got curious."

He took another step. Teresa's eyes blurred with terrified tears. She tried again to pull the trigger. She felt paralyzed. How could she shoot a man? She'd never even hit a dog.

"Sorry he's not home," Lou continued. "I really didn't mean to bother you again. My business is with him, not you. But you're how I found him. See, the school had your address. You fit right in, Miss Lopez, but people saw your gringo boyfriend, and they remembered him. Not too many redheads in Mexico."

He took one more step. "You're not gonna shoot, I know—"

Teresa broke her paralysis with a desperate effort of will and yanked the trigger, forgetting everything Corky had told her about steady hands and smooth motion. The pistol swung wildly as the firing pin snapped down.

The gunshot was tremendously loud in that quiet, dark room. The revolver jumped in her hand like a beast and she almost lost her grip on it. The stab of flame from the muzzle of the gun dazzled her eyes. She smelled gunpowder and smoke.

"As soon as you can, bring the barrel back on target and give him two more shots," James said in her memory. Teresa saw only dark blurs. The gun's flash and smoke had wrecked her night vision. She leveled the pistol where she thought Lou was and fired again.

"Bitch!"

Something struck her on the side of the head. Her ears ringing, Teresa spun clean around. She hit the bed with her knee and fell over. Her cheek felt hot and swollen. She tasted copper in her mouth and knew she was bleeding. Dimly, she saw Lou lunging for her. He wasn't holding the hook anymore. He'd hit her with his fist.

She realized she still had the gun in her left hand. She brought it around and pulled the trigger.

He was a little too fast for her, grabbing her wrist and forcing her hand up. The blast of the gun was right next to both their heads as he drove her down into the mattress. His knee, with the full weight of his body behind it, slammed into her stomach. Breath whooshed out of her lungs with a gasping sob. The gun clattered to the floor.

Lou flinched and put a hand to his face. Blood, dark in the moonlight, streamed down the side of his neck. "You shot me," he said, sounding more surprised than angry. "You stupid bitch."

Teresa tried to struggle, tried to breathe. Her ears were ringing from the gunshot. She clawed at him with her free hand, trying to scratch his eyes. He snatched her other wrist and held her there, still leaning his weight on her belly. She was suffocating.

Lou leaned in. She smelled garlic on his breath. "I'm gonna hurt you for that," he promised. "I'm gonna take my sweet time with you."

Teresa tried to scream, but couldn't get enough air. She saw flashing spots dancing in front of her eyes, and behind them, Lou's eerily calm, terrifying face, only a few inches away.

With the last of her strength, she flung her head forward and rammed her forehead into his nose.

Lou gave a howl of shock and pain. His knee dug even deeper into her stomach for an instant, making Teresa give a gasping moan that was the closest to a scream she could manage. Then he rolled off her, losing his grip on her wrists. He clapped both hands to his face. Blood streamed through his fingers.

Teresa curled involuntarily, coughing and gasping. With watering eyes, she saw Lou stagger back from the bed. He was looking around the room for something. He found it, stooped, and came up again with his hook.

She sucked in a huge breath of air and scrabbled at the nightstand. Her fingers closed around the reading lamp. She threw it at him. The cord caught in the socket for an instant, the lamp swinging crazily. Lou deflected it with his forearm and it crashed to the floor, the bulb shattering.

Teresa rolled off the bed as Lou swung at her. The hook caught the bedsheet and jerked it toward him. She landed on her backside and skidded away on her bare feet, her back slamming against the bedroom wall.

She was cornered. Lou pulled the sheet free of his hook and stared down at her. He was breathing hard, panting harshly. His breathing had a liquid, bubbling quality from his bleeding nose. The side of his head was scorched from the muzzle blast of the point-blank revolver shot and bleeding where her third bullet had grazed him. His right arm was bloody. She must have hit him with the first or second shot, too.

"Okay, that does it," he rasped, and his voice had lost its madman's calm. "I'm gonna hook out your eyes, God damn you, and hang you with a hook through your skull, let you choke on it."

There was a squeal of brakes just outside the house. Lou paused and blinked. Then he swiped the back of his hand under his nose, wiping away some of the blood.

"Time's up, babe," he said, and gave her that empty, psychotic, false-friendly smile. "I'm gonna enjoy this." He walked toward her.

Footsteps rattled on the stairs, coming closer with unbelievable speed. Lou paused again and started to turn toward the bedroom door.

James Corcoran exploded into the room. Teresa had known he was fast, but she'd never imagined a man could move so quickly. Lou swung the hook at him, but the Irishman dipped one shoulder and sidestepped with the grace of a born dancer.

His hand came up, knife flashing. Lou somehow got his other arm in the way and took a slash on the forearm.

James dropped to a crouch, anticipating Lou's backhand swing almost before it began. He let the hook whistle harmlessly over his head and drove his knife into Lou's abdomen, just under the ribcage. The wickedly sharp blade went in all the way to the handle.

Lou grunted like he'd been punched. He froze in place, as if he couldn't quite believe what had just happened.

James yanked his knife free on his way up. His hand moved in a blur, jamming the weapon into the soft spot on the underside of Lou's chin. The blade disappeared from sight, stabbing right up into the Italian's skull.

Lou slowly collapsed to his knees, then onto his face. As the man fell, James tugged his knife back into his hand. He stood there for a second, catching his breath. Fishhook Lou lay very still, blood pooling from his head and belly.

"Are you hurt?" James asked Teresa.

She shook her head numbly.

"Christ on His bloody cross," he said, staring down at Lou's body. "*That* gobshite again?"

"Is he... dead?" Teresa whispered.

"Aye, he's done," James said. "Come, let's get you cleaned up."

*   *   *

The honking horns of the Manhattan traffic stirred Teresa out of her memory. The Oldsmobile crawled ever so slowly. She clenched her hands into fists. She was so close. She'd come all the way across the country and now, less than a mile from her goal, she was stuck. She was tempted to kick open the car door, jump down to the sidewalk, and start running.

That would be stupid, for all sorts of reasons. But it was still tempting.

Norma reached over and patted her hand. "It's all right, dear," she said. "We'll get there."

"We've a long way to go," Teresa said hollowly.

"What was that, dear?"

She shook her head. "Just something James said when we met."

"Do you love him?"

"He saved my life," she said quietly.

Chapter 14

"What happened?" Teresa asked.

James scrubbed at his hands and wrists. The water in the sink turned briefly red, then pink. "I was hoping you'd tell me," he said.

"Lou... how could he possibly know?" she asked.

"Did he say anything?"

"He said something about... coyotes, I think. About how he knew some of the same people they did. And something about a redheaded foreigner."

James's shoulders sagged. "Mother Mary," he muttered. "I didn't bloody think. This is my fault. Again."

"What is? James, we've got a dead man in the bedroom! What do we do?"

"And a car on your front lawn," he added, pulling himself together. "Aye, the coppers will be here soon, if anyone thought to call them. Even around here, gunshots in the dark and reckless driving attract the law. No fear of that, I know how to handle them. But I'd best not be covered in blood when I go out to meet them. You'll stay inside. We'll need to put him in the tub. I can manage, but he's a big lad. It'll go easier if you get his feet. Can you do that?"

Teresa nodded shakily. They went back to the bedroom. James picked up Lou by the shoulders and she got his ankles. Together, they wrestled him into the tub. His dead weight was heavy and awkward, like he was trying to slip through their hands. They left a lot of blood on the floor.

Flashing blue lights strobed through the blinds. They heard people talking in Spanish on the street. James quickly gave his hands another wash.

"I'd best get down there," he said. "Don't let anyone else in. Hide the revolver and get started cleaning the floor. I'll be back as soon as I can."

Teresa felt numb and disconnected. She knew she was in shock. It made everything feel dreamlike and unreal. She went to the broom closet and got a mop. Then, as she started mechanically wiping up Lou's blood, she dimly heard James talking to a policeman. The conversation was quiet and surprisingly courteous. It went on for about fifteen minutes, by which time she'd cleaned all the bloodstains she could find. She stowed the revolver back in the nightstand and swept up the broken bulb from the lamp. It felt good having something to do.

James came back inside and climbed the stairs. He nodded approvingly.

"Well done, Terry. I'll take care of the body."

"What did you tell the police?"

"Oh, I told them I was the worse for drink and misjudged the curb. I explained the noises as a backfiring engine. When I explained it was my own home, there wasn't much else to be said."

"Except you just confessed to driving drunk."

He shrugged. "A first offense in Mexico's no great thing. Twenty hours' incarceration and a fine. I paid the fine up front, and they agreed to waive the jail time."

"So you bribed the cops."

"Bribery's an ugly word. I resolved the situation with a minimum of fuss and red tape."

"You ran the car into our yard?"

"I was in a hurry," he said and shrugged. "Clipped the wall and took some paint off, but no great loss."

"Why were you driving so fast?"

"On the way home, I stopped off to call one of my lads back in New York. I thought I'd best check up on the situation there. He told me everything was fine with you, the whole world still thought you were dead, but word on the street was I'd gone to Mexico. That wasn't supposed to be common knowledge, so I asked around a bit. I found out someone else had been asking about me, and someone had seen me around Playas de Rosarito."

He sighed. "In my line of work, Terry, people only want to find you for two reasons. Either they want to hire you for something, or they want to kill you. As soon as I heard I was blown, I ran back to my car and drove here like a bloody lunatic. All the way I was telling myself you were fine, but I'd no way of knowing for sure and couldn't convince myself. Then, when I got close, I saw a car I didn't know outside, and a flash from the bedroom that looked like gunfire. So I didn't bother with a neat parking job, I just crashed the gate and ran for it."

"You were just in time," she said. "He was going to kill me."

"I know. You did a grand job holding him off."

"You killed him."

"Aye. He'd have done for the both of us if I hadn't."

"I thought... I mean, I knew you were a gangster. But... you kill people." She stared at him. "He wasn't your first, was he?"

His jaw worked silently. He looked down at his own feet.

"I'm glad he's dead," she said, spitting the words out. "He was an awful man. But this isn't how it's supposed to happen."

"Nay, it's not," he said quietly. "Not to you, Terry. You've done more than your share. I'll take care of the rest of this matter, and you needn't concern yourself. Do you think you can sleep?"

"Sleep?" she echoed, an edge of hysterical laughter creeping into her voice. "*Now?*"

"I thought not. Go down to the kitchen and pour yourself some tequila. As large a shot as you think you can manage, neat. Drink it. It'll help."

"Okay," she said. Then, thinking of the kitchen, she blurted out, "There's empanadas in the fridge."

He smiled thinly at that. "Oh? Grand. I'll have one once I've taken care of things."

*   *   *

"Taking care of things" meant smuggling Lou's body out of the house. James got a tarp from the car. He moved the vehicle back to the street and made sure no one was still hanging around watching it. Aside from a bright streak of metal where he'd scraped off the paint against the wall, it was more or less intact. He also turned off the light on the front step, leaving the building draped in shadows. Then he went back upstairs. Teresa watched him from the kitchen. He came down again, staggering under the weight of a rolled-up rug in which, presumably, was Lou. He dragged it out to the car and put it in the trunk. Then he ducked back inside.

"I've seen no sign of any other lads," he said. "I'm thinking he was alone and we're safe enough for the next few hours. I'm just going to take a quick trip down the road. I'll be back in an hour, I promise."

She wanted to scream at him not to leave, that she couldn't be alone anymore, especially not tonight; not for an hour, not for ten minutes.

"Okay," was what she said.

He was back fifty-three minutes later, in a different car, an off-white beat-up Toyota. He didn't tell her where he'd gotten it, or where he'd left their old ride, and she didn't ask. She heated up some empanadas and he ate two, taking swigs of tequila straight from the bottle between bites.

Teresa watched him across the table. She felt him slipping away from her, becoming more distant, more of a stranger. She wanted to reach out to him but didn't know how.

"Well, that's done," he said at last. "The coppers won't find anything. I've talked to another lad. He'll bring a car for you."

"What about the one you've got?" she asked, pointing toward the front door.

"I'll take it north tomorrow morning."

She heard the "you" and "I" he was using instead of "us." His words hung in the air between them.

"Where are you going?" she asked in a small voice.

"New York."

A new jolt of fright spurred her to a desperate lunge. She snatched at his hands across the table, as if she could anchor him in place. "No!"

"I've no choice, Terry."

"Why?"

He looked at her, and in his eyes she saw a deep unhappiness. "I'm putting you in danger every minute I stay here, Terry. This was my affair, and it followed me to you. I've one job to do, to keep you safe, and there's only one way I can do that now. I don't know if Lou told anyone else where I was, but we've got to assume he did. When he doesn't come back, they'll send someone else. Maybe more than one. The Mafia have contacts with the cartels hereabouts. Sooner or later someone will tumble to you, or they'll use you to get to me. Besides, I can't very well be slaying hitmen all the day long. I've got to go back where I'm known, and they've got to know I'm there. That's the only way you'll be safe. Then they'll leave you alone."

"No!" she said again, still holding on.

"I love you, Terry," he said. "And that's why I've got to go."

"We'll figure something out. Together. That's what couples do."

He shook his head. "I'm sorry. For bringing danger to your door. For being the lad I am. I'm not sorry for loving you, though. I'll never forget you."

"Don't you dare," she said. "Don't say goodbye. You don't get to walk away from me. Not now!"

"I'm doing it to save you."

"I don't care why you're doing it!" She squeezed his hands. "Don't go. It won't help, not in the end. I'm supposed to be with you."

"You can't save me, Teresa."

"I'm the only one who can," she said. "If you go back to your old life, it'll kill you."

"Maybe." He tried a lopsided smile. "But I've always been lucky."

"I won't let you go."

"This isn't yours to choose any more than it's mine, love. I'll not have you die because of me."

Teresa was crying, big tears rolling down her cheeks. "If you go to New York, I'll follow you there."

"Don't you dare," he said, echoing her. "Not until the trial. Vitelli's got too many friends. Remember why you left."

"Then I'll come for you after he's locked up for good," she said. "You're not walking away from me forever, James Corcoran."

He studied her face. "Nay," he said. "I suppose I'm not. Here. It's against all reason and sense, but that's never stopped me before. I'll get you a phone, one that only I know the number for. I'll keep in touch, let you know I'm all right. I'll check up on you, whenever I can. And I promise, I'll not keep company with another lass while we're parted. Not one. Fair enough?"

It wasn't what she wanted. It wasn't even close. But she could see it wasn't what he wanted, either, and that somehow made it a little easier to bear. "Okay," she said. "You win."

"I've won plenty of times in my life," he said bitterly. "This isn't what winning feels like. It feels like the worst hand of cards the Fates could've dealt us. But sometimes if you're dealt a bad hand, the best you can do is avoid losing for a while. Or bluff like a right bastard. And now we'd best get some sleep. You've a job to go to, and I've a trip to make."

"Not yet," she said.

"Terry, it's late, and we've said everything there is to say."

"Then stop talking," she said. "If all we've got is memory for the next few months, we'd better make it memorable. Take me upstairs and make love to me."

It wasn't soft or tender, not this time. They clung to each other as if they were drowning, trying to draw every scrap of comfort they could from the connection of their bodies. Teresa clutched at him, her fingers drawing red lines on his arms and back. She kissed him hard and tasted blood from her split lip. At the final, shattering end, she gasped, gave a little scream, and collapsed shuddering onto the bed, in tears. He held her, she held him, and she thought that maybe, if they didn't let go, they could keep the outside world away. If not forever, at least for one more night.

*   *   *

Teresa woke knowing something was wrong. She opened her eyes and found herself alone. The room was dark. James's pillow still held the impression of his head, but the sheets were cool to the touch.

"James?" she asked quietly. Then, louder, "James!"

She heard his familiar footsteps on the stairs and sagged back in relief. What a terrible dream she'd had.

He turned on the light and stood there in the doorway with his usual easy, charming smile on his face. He seemed relaxed, pleasant, calm. But she saw the tightness around his eyes and the shadows under them. Her halfhearted attempt to dismiss what had happened fell apart.

"Is it time?" she whispered.

"Aye, it's time. I've a few things for you, before I go. I've been out and about while you've been sleeping. I've acquired another car. It's a blue Nissan, parked out front."

"You didn't steal it, did you?"

He looked wounded. "Of course not! Elena Lopez is a good, law-abiding woman. I'd not tarnish her record. It's bought and paid for. I've left the keys on the dining table, together with the title and a burner phone."

"Burner?"

"Prepaid, disposable, bought with cash. No one can trace it to you. Keep a charge in it and keep it about you. I'll call when I can, generally in the early evening. If you don't hear from me every day, you needn't fret. But I'll check in with you once a week at the very least."

She got out of bed and started pulling clothes on. "Have you eaten anything?"

"No need to trouble yourself, love. I can get something on the road."

"James, I'm not letting you start a trip without giving you breakfast. My mom would never forgive me."

"You think your mum would approve of everything we've been up to?" he asked, raising an eyebrow.

"Probably not," Teresa allowed. Then she flinched. "James, we... we killed a man last night. We really did. We're... murderers."

He crossed the room in three quick strides, putting his hands on her shoulders. "Terry, we'd no choice. He'd have killed the both of us, you know that. Besides, the hurt you did to him wouldn't have killed him. If you need to blame someone, the fault's mine. You're no murderer."

"I don't blame you, James," she said, forcing a smile. "You've only ever been trying to protect me. If it wasn't for me, you wouldn't have even been here."

"And I'd be the poorer for it," he replied with a more genuine smile. "Well, if you insist, I'd not object to an omelet, western-style, and a tequila sunrise."

"Just one," she said. "You're not driving drunk."

"Terry," he said, putting a hand on her cheek. "Whatever am I going to do without you to take care of me?"

"I hope you'll be a little more careful. Luck only gets you so far. You have to promise me, you won't get yourself killed before I see you again."

"What about after?" he asked with the mischievous twinkle she'd come to know so well.

"Not then, either."

"All right, love, I promise I'll take no unnecessary risks."

That would have to be good enough, Teresa knew. She finished buttoning her blouse and slipped into her shoes. The two of them went downstairs to the kitchen. She cracked four eggs into the frying pan and started cooking. James mixed the drinks.

"There's an extra box of shells for your revolver," he said, pointing to a cardboard box next to the keys and phone. "I'd recommend taking it out of town and practicing a bit, just in case. Blow a few holes in some tin cans, get so you can hit what you're aiming at. But I've a notion you won't be bothered again, not once I'm away. And there's a bank book. I've opened an account in your name. I know you've an income of your own, but I'll transfer some petty cash on occasion, just to make sure you're not wanting for anything."

"James?"

"Aye?"

"Thank you."

"It was a mad idea of Erin's to rope me into this scheme in the first place." He grinned at her. "But I'm rather glad she did."

"Because you wouldn't have gotten involved in any mad schemes on your own," she said with a straight face.

After breakfast, she walked him out to his Toyota. He took his duffel bag with him, but had left some of his clothes behind, explaining he liked to travel light. She didn't mind. Having some tangible evidence of him nearby would help, some. It might help her believe she'd see him again. The sky was a deep, velvety blue, just turning pink away to the east. She smelled the sea and tasted salt on her lips.

"I'll call you from the road," he promised. "Once I'm over the border, I'll ring you from the airport. I'll be flying from San Diego to New York."

She put her arms around him one more time. "I love you, James."

He kissed her lightly. "And I love you, Terry. No fear, it's not goodbye forever."

* * *

"Here we are," Mark said. He brought the Oldsmobile to a halt in front of the hospital entrance.

"Thank you," Teresa said hurriedly, unbuckling her seatbelt. "Thank you so much. You've been so kind to me!"

"You're very welcome, dear," Norma said. "And it was very nice meeting you. I hope everything works out with you and your young man. God bless you."

Mark already had the trunk open. He insisted on getting her back out for her. She didn't argue. Her heart was fluttering in her chest. She was wondering, now, what she'd see in James's hospital bed. Would it be the cocky, charismatic man who had guided her, guarded her, and won her heart? Or would it be a broken, pitiful shell?

She squared her shoulders. If James had taught her one thing, it was how to be brave. She would face whatever she had to. She could still love him, no matter what had been done to him. Of that she had no doubt.

Teresa picked up her suitcase and started walking toward the hospital doors. They slid open to welcome her in.

Chapter 15

It wasn't the life Teresa wanted, but as the days went by, she found herself more contented than she'd expected. She loved the kids—*her* kids, she'd come to think of them—and looked forward to school. She made friends with several of the families and was invited to dinners, birthday parties, and one older sibling's *quinceanera*. A couple of the women, with careful diplomacy, asked what had happened to that nice American man she'd been seeing, but accepted her answer that he'd had to go back to the United States for work. Several of them had husbands who were working north of the border, after all, sending money back to them, and many of those were involved in illegal enterprises. They understood.

No other alarming men came sniffing around. James had called her the first night, and almost every night thereafter. He told her his homecoming was well known in the East Coast underworld, so anyone wanting James Corcoran would be headed to New York rather than Mexico. She would be in no more danger on his account.

She thrived on their conversations. The lilt of his Irish brogue was the finest sound Teresa knew, guaranteed to melt her heart. He was always cheerful, always glad to talk to her. He did manage to communicate that her family, though understandably devastated by her "death," was otherwise getting by.

"I know a lad in the undertaker's trade," he said. "And he knows the lad who presided over your burial. It was a grand occasion, so they tell me. Sad music, heartfelt testimonials, the lot. They didn't make a sound recording, but I've a few photos I can send, if you'd like."

"Photos? Of my own funeral? Isn't that a little morbid?"

"Aye," he cheerfully agreed. "And I've seen the tombstone. It's very fine. Engraved and everything. We'll visit it together, one of these days."

He also transferred money to her bank account—an embarrassingly large amount by local standards. She didn't spend much of it, being a saver by nature. It was good to have an emergency nest egg, just in case.

Teresa did get the sense that something was on James's mind. He became a little preoccupied, a little more guarded in his conversation. She gathered it had something to do with his work, but he didn't volunteer anything and she didn't ask.

One night, several weeks after he'd gone back to New York, he called her just after six, West Coast time. Fortunately, the difference in their time zones didn't matter much to a night owl like James.

After the usual exchange of pleasantries and endearments, he said something odd.

"It's possible I may be changing the focus of my occupation, love."

"What do you mean?" she asked.

"You'll recall the lass who introduced us to one another?"

Teresa almost blurted out, "You mean Detective O'Reilly?" She stopped herself, remembering that he'd told her to be careful about anything surrounding the detective's double life. "Yes," was what she said.

"I don't want you drawing the wrong conclusions, but she and I have been working on something important. It's likely you and I may be in similar circumstances in the not-too-distant future."

Teresa frowned as she tried to puzzle that out. Then it hit her.

"Oh my God," she murmured. "You mean that, James? You're getting out of the Life? For good?"

"Aye," he said. "It'll be a mite difficult, and may be some time in the making, but we'll be closing a deal that... well, love, I hope you'll be proud of me."

"I'm already proud of you, James."

"Now, if you'll excuse me, I've some other business to be about."

"Of course. I love you."

"You're my special lass. If you're still up, I may call you again later this evening."

"I'll wait up for you," she promised.

*   *   *

James didn't call.

Teresa had a lesson plan to finish. She finished it. She took a nice, long bath and managed not to think too much about Lou's body getting stuffed into the tub. She tried to concentrate on a book, the sort of guilty-pleasure bodice-ripping romance novel she'd never admit to reading.

And she thought about what James had told her. He was working with the police on some sort of deal. Was he about to go into witness protection? That must have been what he'd meant by "similar circumstances."

She wasn't sure how she felt about that. Obviously, she didn't like that James was a criminal. God, she'd gotten into this mess in the first place because she'd needed to hide from people like him! No, that wasn't quite right. James wasn't a murderer like the man she'd agreed to testify against.

Except that he'd murdered a man right there in their bedroom. And she'd helped him do it.

It wasn't like that, she told herself and almost believed it. She did believe he'd never do anything to hurt her. And she believed he loved her.

James had to be one of the last people in North America who still used pay phones. But he also used a burner cell, and its number was in her call history. As the evening wore on, Teresa found herself looking at the phone log. What would it hurt? She'd just drop him a quick line.

She was hitting the call-back button before she could talk herself out of it. He probably wouldn't answer. He was likely on his "other business" and wouldn't even have the phone on his person. Maybe it would even be turned off. She'd let it ring six times, then hang up, she decided. She perched on the edge of her bed and listened to the rhythmic ring of the phone.

On the fifth ring, the line opened. She expected James's breezy "Evening, love."

There was silence on the other end of the line, except for some faint background noises she couldn't identify. She heard distant, indistinct voices and some other sounds.

"Hello?" she said tentatively.

"Who is this?" a man's voice answered.

Teresa sat back and caught her breath. That wasn't James. It was a heavier voice, rougher, with a Long Island accent, the kind of voice she'd heard a lot growing up. It sounded like a thug.

"Who is this?" the guy said again.

"Who are you?" she whispered.

"Lady, this is the NYPD. Identify yourself."

She felt like she'd been punched in the stomach. Why would the police be answering James's phone? There had to be another reason, something less awful than what was going through her head.

Teresa tried to speak around the enormous lump in her throat. "I... I need to talk to Detective O'Reilly," she managed to say.

"What was that?"

"Detective O'Reilly," she said, louder. "Erin O'Reilly."

"Just a second," he said, his voice sounding a little funny. Then she heard him say, "It's some woman, says she'll only talk to you."

"This is Detective O'Reilly," said a familiar female voice.

Teresa was astonished. She'd never expected O'Reilly to be standing right there. What was going on?

"Detective," she said quietly, "it's me."

"Ma'am, I don't have time to screw around," O'Reilly said. "Tell me your name."

"I shouldn't say it. But you know me."

There was a short pause.

"Oh," the detective said. "I see."

There was another pause.

"You shouldn't be calling here," O'Reilly said. "You shouldn't even have this phone number. Where arc... no, never mind. I don't need to know. Why are you calling? Are you in trouble?"

"What's happened to James?" Teresa blurted out. A part of her, a large part, didn't want Detective O'Reilly to answer the question, but an even larger part *needed* that answer.

"James Corcoran was shot earlier this evening."

Shot. The word was so abrupt, so final, like a gunshot itself. Shot. James couldn't have been shot. He was too quick, too lucky. And he was *hers*.

"Is... is he...?" she stammered, somehow getting the words out. She was sure she was going to throw up or faint.

"He's in critical condition at Bellevue," O'Reilly said, in the tone of a professional policewoman who'd often had to inform people of this sort of thing. "He's in surgery right now."

"How badly is he hurt?"

"He's critical," O'Reilly repeated. "It'll be touch and go. We've got a good doc working on him."

"Who shot him?"

"Wiseguys, obviously. They hit him at home, and we think he tagged one of them pretty good. Now, ma'am, you really should get off the line here. Unless there's any information you can give me about what happened?"

"Please," Teresa said, and the way she said it made O'Reilly pause.

"Yeah?"

"Is... is he going to be okay?"

She heard O'Reilly's sigh even over the phone. "Oh God, he wasn't kidding about you, was he. You and he... Jesus. What a mess. Okay, look. I know the surgeon. He's my brother, as a matter of fact. There's no one I'd rather have holding the knife if someone I care about goes on the table. Corky caught two slugs; one in the arm, one in the chest. He's got a collapsed lung, a broken arm, and he'd lost a lot of blood by the time the paramedics got to him. He's damn lucky to be alive. But he made it to the hospital, so I'd say his chances are better than even."

Teresa closed her eyes. "Thank you, Detective."

"Now, you know it's dangerous for you to have any contact with anyone here," O'Reilly said more quietly. "Is this a number you can be reached at?"

"Yes."

"I'll call you in a day or two, let you know how he's doing. Don't call again. Don't do anything. Just hang tight in the meantime, okay?"

"Okay."

"Now we've got to go run down the son of a bitch who did this. I need to go. Talk to you later."

O'Reilly hung up. Teresa sat staring at the phone. Words bounced around her brain. Hang tight, she thought disjointedly. James was shot. Twice. Lost a lot of blood. Chances better than even. Critical condition. They'd call her in a day or two. Shot. Collapsed lung. In surgery.

"No."

Her word echoed in the empty room. She wouldn't do it, *couldn't*. There was no way she could sit here in this little house in Mexico while the man she loved was fighting for his life. How many times had she heard that phrase, without really understanding it? James was *fighting for his life*. And if that was true, she needed to be there with him, fighting beside him. Either one of them would have died on their own against Fishhook Lou. They needed each other.

Teresa made another phone call, to the operator. She asked for the phone number for the San Diego airport. Then she placed that call.

"I need a ticket to New York City," she told the agent. "Any time tomorrow."

"Okay, ma'am," the agent said. "I've got a flight leaving at 8:30 in the morning, nonstop. How many passengers?"

"One."

"Will you be needing a return ticket?"

"No." Teresa was already laying out her clothes, starting to pack.

"What's the name?"

"Elena Lopez."

After she'd finalized the flight info, Teresa hung up. She looked around at the house she'd only just started to think of as home. What she was doing was dangerous, risky, crazy. Detective O'Reilly would have been horrified, would have ordered her not to do it. But O'Reilly wasn't there. Even James might have tried to stop her. But he couldn't stop her; he was too busy *fighting for his life.*

"Hang on," she said. "I'm coming." It was time to go back to New York City. Teresa Tommasino was done running away.

*   *   *

Teresa walked down the hospital corridor. At the end of the hallway was a door. A uniformed police officer sat in a chair outside the door. He looked bored until he saw her coming toward him. Then he stood up and faced her. His hand rested next to the butt of his pistol.

"Ma'am, please stop right there," he said.

Teresa stopped. She was sure, now, she'd come to the right place.

"I think maybe you're lost, ma'am," the cop said.

"I'm here to see James Corcoran," she said.

"He's under police protection. No visitors."

"I just need to see him for a moment. I'm a friend of his."

"Not gonna happen, lady." The officer's face and voice were warier than before. He'd dropped all pretense of friendliness. He was looking at her suitcase.

Teresa was actually glad to see it. The NYPD were taking James's safety seriously. She played her trump card. Slowly, so he wouldn't get the wrong idea, she opened her suitcase and carefully removed her wallet. The cop watched her closely. His hand was actually on his gun now.

"Here's my identification," she said, extending her passport to him, alongside Detective O'Reilly's business card. "My name is Elena Lopez. I'm working with Detective O'Reilly in Major Crimes. We've been working closely with Mr. Corcoran."

The cop put out his left hand and took the papers, without removing his right from the grip of his handgun. He flipped open the passport and did a quick comparison with her face.

"I gotta call this in," he said.

"By all means," she said.

"Don't move, ma'am." The officer keyed his radio, keeping his eyes on her. "This is Beaufort, down at Bellevue, on the Corcoran protection detail. Shield six-two-oh-eight."

"Go ahead, Beaufort," Dispatch replied.

"I got a female civilian here, name of Elena Lopez, wants to see Corcoran. Says she's working with Major Crimes. She's got O'Reilly's card."

"Stand by." The dispatch operator made some connections. "Okay, you're patched through to O'Reilly."

"O'Reilly?"

"Go ahead," Detective O'Reilly said through the radio.

"This is Beaufort, at Bellevue. Got a woman wants to talk to our guy. Says her name's Lopez, but I dunno... looks more Italian than Mexican to me. I'm gettin' a kinda shady vibe off her."

"What's she look like?" O'Reilly asked.

"About five-four, medium build, mid-thirties, black hair. Looks kinda like a schoolteacher, not a wiseguy, you ask me. But she's up to something, I'd bet my shield on it."

Teresa bristled quietly, but she couldn't fault the cop's instincts. After all, he'd pegged her pretty much dead to rights.

O'Reilly didn't reply right away.

"You want me to take her in?" Beaufort asked. "Bring her downtown, run a check?"

"No!" O'Reilly said sharply.

"Copy that," Beaufort said, a little confused. "What do you want me to do with her, then?"

"Ask her something," O'Reilly said. "What car was Corcoran driving the first time she met him?"

Beaufort looked expectantly at Teresa.

For a terrible moment, she couldn't remember. Then recognition flooded back. "A gray Toyota Corolla."

"She's okay," O'Reilly said. "Let her in."

"Copy that. Beaufort out."

He opened the door. "Don't take too long," he added. "He's pretty tired. And don't try anything funny. I'll be watching. You better leave the case out here. I'll keep an eye on it."

Teresa nodded and stepped through the doorway. Beaufort didn't close the door all the way, and she knew he was hovering, just in case. She didn't care. All her attention was on the man in the hospital bed.

James lay on his back, eyes closed. His normally light complexion was sheet white. A tube ran into his mouth. IV tubes snaked out of his arm. His other arm was in a sling. One of those beeping hospital machines was connected to him by a fingertip clip. Teresa saw, with a pang, that his good arm was linked to the bed by a handcuff.

"Oh, James," she whispered, hurrying across the room. She wanted to grab him and hold on as hard as she could, but that was obviously a bad idea. She pulled up short at his bedside. Then, unable to help herself, she touched his good hand.

He opened his eyes. They were blurred and unfocused. He blinked a couple of times and turned his head toward her. When he saw her, his eyes lit up. He couldn't speak, but he squeezed her hand lightly. He asked a question with his eyes.

Teresa leaned close and whispered to him. "It's okay, James. I'm back. I'm Elena Lopez, remember? No one's looking for me. It's you they want. Oh God, James, what did they do to you?"

The corners of his eyes crinkled with a smile his mouth couldn't make. He managed the slightest apologetic shrug of his shoulders as if to say, what could you do?

"I've been thinking," she went on, hoping the cop outside couldn't hear her. "Are you under arrest?"

He jiggled the handcuffed wrist, then shook his head.

"You'll be out of here soon," she went on. "When you are, you're going to need someone to help you out at home. A live-in nurse, maybe?"

He nodded.

"Well, Elena Lopez was thinking about picking up a nursing certification to go with her teaching credentials," she said. "I'm sure someone could put the paperwork together, if he knew a guy."

There was that twinkle in his eye that she'd missed so much. He winked, held her hand a little tighter, and nodded.

"I'm going to take care of you, James," she said. "I told you, I'm the only one who can save you. And I'm going to. I don't care what you've done. I care who you are. Your mom said there never was a Corcoran who amounted to anything. Well, she didn't hang around long enough to find out. You're more than anything, James Corcoran. You're everything. To me."

She bent over him and carefully, gently kissed his cheek. She tasted salt on her lips and saw he had tears in his eyes.

He let go of her hand. She was confused for a moment, but then she saw he was making scribbling motions. Teresa's boarding pass was in her pocket. There was a clipboard at the base of the bed with a pen tied to it by a piece of string. She handed them to him.

Writing wasn't easy for him. She held the paper against his thigh as he painstakingly wrote out a single sentence. She recognized it. He'd remembered one of the first things he'd ever said to her.

We've a long way to go, and plenty of time for talking.

"You're right, James," she said, praying it was true. "We've got plenty of time."

Ready for more?

Join the Clickworks Press email list
for the latest on new releases, upcoming books and
series, behind-the-scenes details, events, and more.

Be the first to know about new releases in the Erin
O'Reilly Mysteries by signing up at
clickworkspress.com/join/erin

About the Author

Steven Henry learned how to read almost before he learned how to walk. Ever since he began reading stories, he wanted to put his own on the page. He lives a very quiet and ordinary life in Minnesota with his wife and dog.

Also by Steven Henry

Fathers
A Modern Christmas Story

When you strip away everything else, what's left is the truth

Life taught Joe Davidson not to believe in miracles. A blue-collar woodworker, Joe is trying to build a future. His father drank himself to death and his mother succumbed to cancer, leaving a broken, struggling family. He and his brother and sisters are faced with failed marriages, growing pains, and lingering trauma.

Then a chance meeting at his local diner brings Mary Elizabeth Reynolds into his life. Suddenly, Joe finds himself reaching for something more, a dream of happiness. The wood-worker and the poor girl from a trailer park connect and fall in love, and for a little while, everything is right with their world.

But suddenly Joe is confronted with a situation he never imagined. What do you do if your fiancée is expecting a child you know isn't yours? Torn between betrayal and love, trying to do the right thing when nothing seems right anymore, Joe has to strip life down to its truth and learn that, in spite of the pain, love can be the greatest miracle of all.

Learn more at clickworkspress.com/fathers.

Ember of Dreams

The Clarion Chronicles, Book One

When magic awakens a long-forgotten folk, a noble lady, a young apprentice, and a solitary blacksmith band together to prevent war and seek understanding between humans and elves.

Lady Kristyn Tremayne – An otherwise unremarkable young lady's open heart and inquisitive mind reveal a hidden world of magic.

Robert Blackford – A humble harp maker's apprentice dreams of being a hero.

Master Gabriel Zane – A master blacksmith's pursuit of perfection leads him to craft an enchanted sword, drawing him out of his isolation and far from his cozy home.

Lord Luthor Carnarvon – A lonely nobleman with a dark past has won the heart of Kristyn's mother, but at what cost?

Readers love *Ember of Dreams*

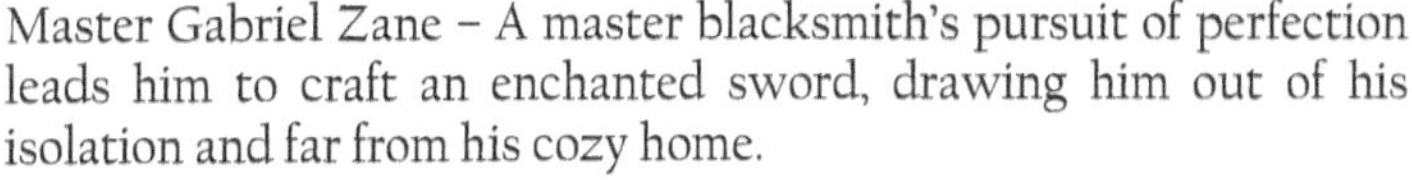

"The more I got to know the characters, the more I liked them. The female lead in particular is a treat to accompany on her journey from ordinary to extraordinary."

"The author's deep understanding of his protagonists' motivations and keen eye for psychological detail make Robert and his companions a likable and memorable cast."

Learn more at tinyurl.com/emberofdreams.

More great titles from Clickworks Press

www.clickworkspress.com

The Altered Wake

Megan Morgan

Amid growing unrest, a family secret and an ancient laboratory unleash long-hidden superhuman abilities. Now newly-promoted Sentinel Cameron Kardell must chase down a rogue superhuman who holds the key to the powers' origin: the greatest threat Cotarion has seen in centuries – and Cam's best friend.

"Incredible. Starts out gripping and keeps getting better."

Learn more at clickworkspress.com/sentinel1.

Hubris Towers: The Complete First Season

Ben Y. Faroe & Bill Hoard

Comedy of manners meets comedy of errors in a new series for fans of Fawlty Towers and P. G. Wodehouse.

"So funny and endearing"

"Had me laughing so hard that I had to put it down to catch my breath"

"Astoundingly, outrageously funny!"

Learn more at clickworkspress.com/hts01.

Death's Dream Kingdom
Gabriel Blanchard

A young woman of Victorian London has been transformed into a vampire. Can she survive the world of the immortal dead— or perhaps, escape it?

"The wit and humor are as Victorian as the setting... a winsomely vulnerable and tremendously crafted work of art."

"A dramatic, engaging novel which explores themes of death, love, damnation, and redemption."

Learn more at clickworkspress.com/ddk.

Share the love!

Join our microlending team at
kiva.org/team/clickworkspress.

Keep in touch!

Join the Clickworks Press email list
and get freebies, production updates, special deals,
behind-the-scenes sneak peeks, and more.

Sign up today at clickworkspress.com/join.